DEATH IS IN THE DETAILS

HEATHER SUNSERI

SUN PUBLISHING

Heather Sunseri/Sun Publishing
PO Box 1264
Versailles, Kentucky 40383
https://heathersunseri.com

Cover design by Jessica Bell
Edited by David Gatewood

DEATH IS IN THE DETAILS/ Heather Sunseri. -- 1st ed.

ALSO BY HEATHER SUNSERI

THE EMERGE SERIES

Emerge

Uprising

Renaissance

The Meeting (A short story)

ONE

A nother fire roared to life as the bodies of two parents cooled across town.

I incorporated the sound of my buzzing phone into my dream at predawn hours. I was five years old and cooking with my mom. We were mixing dough to make cutout cookies. The buzzing? An electric mixer—the kind you hold in your hand and with beaters you can lick after.

The sweet scent of vanilla permeated the air. A fire burned in the fireplace, crackling and popping as fire met sap.

The soothing buzzing stopped, replaced by a violent bang.

My eyes shot open, and I gasped. My heart beat wildly. I was not in my childhood home, and my mom was still dead, a memory that rushed back like it had just happened.

With tears running into my hairline from the flood of memories, I stared up from my bed at the golden light that danced along the curved walls and ceiling of my 1969 Airstream—a trailer renovated and situated in the middle of a twenty-acre piece of farmland I grew up on, land I inherited when my mother was brutally murdered and I nearly burned to death.

Sitting up slowly, careful not to make a sound, I took in the flickering light of five votive candles in glass jars sitting on a shelf built around my queen-size bed. Candles I had *not* lit. Goose bumps sprang up on my limbs, and the hairs along the back of my neck stood at full alert.

I listened carefully for whatever had made the banging sound moments before, no easy task with my heart jack-hammering. Had I imagined it?

I certainly wasn't imagining the candlelight that bathed my trailer in a warm, yellow glow and gave it the soothing scent of vanilla.

Outside my bedroom, near the kitchen, Gus, a stray cat that had wandered onto my property last year and decided to grace me with her extended presence, meowed loudly while staring at the door.

My phone began buzzing again. Still partially para-lyzed, I stared at it. It was lying upside down, preventing me from seeing the caller.

A strange scratching noise came from somewhere outside the trailer, and I gripped my comforter with tight fists. I forced my heart rate to slow. Clutching my comforter was not going to keep me alive if there was an intruder here to kill me.

I rolled over and grabbed the Maglight I kept beside the bed—a formidable club of a weapon in a pinch. With the heavy flashlight in my hand, and the minor comfort of knowing that at least the intruder was no longer inside my trailer, I grabbed my phone. "Hello," I said in a low, hushed voice.

"Faith, it's Penelope." She sang brightly like she'd been up for hours—and she probably had. "There's been a fire, sweetie, and they need you there as soon as possible." Only Penelope Champagne, Paynes Creek's finest 911 dispatcher, who also doubled as the receptionist for the Paynes Creek PD, could make the announcement of a crime sound like an invitation to breakfast. *Faith, honey, you're invited to Bryn's Coffeehouse for cinnamon rolls. See you in ten.*

"Okay," I said, still barely above a whisper, as I climbed out of bed. Penelope didn't seem to notice I was speaking in a low voice. Something stopped me from telling her about my not-so-romantic candlelit trailer. "I take it there's more to it than just a fire?" I made my way into the other part of the trailer with the flashlight held over my head, ready to strike. I could take this call *and* defend myself and my home.

Gus looked up at me and yawned, then turned back to face the door. She wasn't usually this interested in people coming and going, except maybe when my brother and his wife or my aunt and uncle stopped by. But Gus wouldn't dream of hissing or getting loud with Aunt Leah—who often brought her treats—or my sister-in-law. She did sometimes get territorial with Uncle Henry or my brother Finch. She acted more like a guard dog than an ambivalent cat.

Once I'd confirmed that there was no one in the trailer, I lowered the flashlight. I thought about having Penelope send a uniform out to check things out, but I knew it would be pointless, and everyone at the station already thought I was crazy after the last time I called and said someone had been inside my trailer. They found no sign of forced entry. Nothing was missing. All I could say was that I knew things had been moved around.

And they had been. My clothes had been rearranged. The knives in my kitchen were in a different drawer. My bed, which had been left unmade that morning, was made, and pillows were arranged differently. And a bouquet of daisies with a yellow satin bow adorned the bed.

The officers at the station didn't think I heard the things they said behind my back. They thought I didn't know they had a betting pool going to see who could get me to go out on a date first—or worse, get me in the sack. Yes, they thought I was certifiable, but the more egocentric ones still viewed me as a puzzle to be solved—a woman with a dark past who needed to be conquered. Not to mention, as I overheard once, they considered me "entirely bangable." And then there were the rare nice guys, but they all seemed to think they might be able to "fix" me. After all, if Chief Reid saw enough sane and good in me to hire me for my services, I must not be an entirely lost cause. But even the nice guys inevitably found me to be too much work.

All of that combined to keep me from mentioning the burning candles to Penelope. I knew someone was messing with me, but not who, and for all I knew it could even be one of the police officers. Maybe they'd discovered the significance of the white daisies.

Or maybe that was just a lucky guess.

Penelope explained the crime scene I was being called to. "Apparent murder-suicide, but it could also be arson. Chief wants you there to document the scene so they can move the bodies before more press shows up."

"Meaning?" I asked.

"You know the Reynolds girl? The teenager that Mr. Lake, the orchestra teacher, was supposedly having a relationship with? It's her parents' home—they're the two victims. The daughter hasn't been located. That poor child. They arrested Mr. Lake yesterday for sexual misconduct with a minor, but his attorneys got him out before the ink had dried on his fingerprints."

From outside the trailer, I caught the distinct sound of a crackling wood fire. I turned and looked out the back window. A bonfire raged in my fire pit, about forty yards away.

"Faith? Did you hear me?" Penelope asked. "You ready for the address?"

The fire was large and beautiful, set by someone who knew what they were doing. Large enough to strike awe without being a danger to spread out of control, and small enough to sit beside it in the Adirondack chairs or on the thick logs surrounding the pit. And this wasn't the first time in recent weeks that someone had started a fire there.

"Yeah," I said. "Text me the address."

I hung up and stared out at the fire. Once upon a time I would get lost in the flames of a fire like this. They fascinated me. The way yellow, orange, white, and blue intertwined like silky-smooth hair. But I wasn't fascinated now. Now my eyes weren't drawn to the golden blaze, but to the dark figure standing next to it.

I could just make out the profile of a man. At least I thought it was a man. Tall, pointed nose, baseball cap. A bulky jacket that made him look like he had a beer gut. Or maybe he was just overweight.

I could only stand there and stare, paralyzed. My heart tightened, and I didn't breathe for several beats. Gus weaved figure eights through my legs.

Then the figure turned, and though the fire backlit him, and I couldn't see his eyes, I knew he was looking straight at me.

A lump formed in my throat. Even if I wanted to scream, I couldn't.

I thought about calling Penelope back. Or my brother. Anyone. Just so that someone could see that I wasn't crazy.

Instead, I spun toward the front door. My sudden

movement sent Gus sprinting to the back of the trailer. I flew down the steps and raced around the front of the Airstream. I would face this man who was stalking me, taunting me, making me question my sanity even more than usual.

But I was not to discover the stranger's identity today. Because by the time I turned the corner and faced the fire pit, the figure had vanished. And all I was left with was a blaze reminiscent of a past impossible to forget—a miniature version of my own slice of hell.

TWO

The rope wasn't long enough to have been used for a hanging.

That was my first thought as I snapped pictures of the crime scene that morning. But as a forensic photographer, my job was to document, not investigate.

Penelope had called this an apparent murder-suicide. *Apparent.* That's what news reporters liked to call it when they got unsubstantiated "tips" surrounding an investigation. In this case, it was "apparent" that a man had hanged himself, according to Chief Reid. And because the man's wife was also dead, it was presumed that he must have killed her first.

And then the entire house had burned down.

But who or what had started the fire? Did the husband start the fire before killing himself? Or was it accidental? Had they left a candle burning? A pot on the stove?

I snapped a photo of the charred rope lying loosely against the man's neck. Looked for more rope, but didn't find any. This was no hanging, in my opinion.

The part of this couple's story that was so heart-breaking involved the teenager they'd left behind: Bella Reynolds, a seventeen-year-old at the center of Paynes Creek's latest scandal. Days away from being eighteen— not that that would make a relationship with a teacher any less inappropriate. And now, not only had she been emotionally violated, not only was she being gossiped about by just about every bored housewife and teenage kid in town, but she would have to face it all without her parents.

I knew what that was like. Rumors still surrounded the circumstances of my mom's and her husband's deaths— rumors and speculation about what had caused my step-brother Ethan to snap. It was hard to believe that it was only twelve years ago that he was charged, and later convicted, of murdering both my mom and his father before burning down my childhood home with both victims inside.

So, yeah, I knew what Bella was facing.

I moved around and snapped a different angle of the rope. I placed a measuring stick alongside the rope in order to give scale.

Staring at the bodies of Bella's parents, I vowed not to become personally vested in whatever had happened here. For me, this would be nothing more than another bad day, a convenient distraction. A way to temporarily cloud those memories I could never forget—literally. I suffered from hyperthymesia, which meant I possessed the highly unusual trait of remembering every single day of my life with near one hundred percent clarity. Just another thing about me that made me "strange." Or, in the eyes of many, mentally ill.

I once attended a high school reunion. I joined in conversations with people I'd known most of my life. But when I shared crystal clear memories of trivial conversations with classmates, or recalled precisely what they were wearing on days in the distant past, I got strange looks. People don't like to be reminded of everything that ever happened. Especially the bad or embarrassing stuff. The past is supposed to fade—or better yet, be misremembered.

For that reason, I'd always tried to keep it a secret that I had hyperthymesia. A few people knew, but not many. Better to just let the rest go on thinking I was weird.

Some people don't mind weird.

Bundled in a thick down coat and covered in protective gear to keep my DNA out of the crime scene, I looked around. It was just after sunrise, and the autumn air had turned colder overnight, made worse by thick clouds that promised to keep the sun from breaking through. The stench of smoke from the burning of wood, plastic, and human flesh drifted up from the soot and ashes and penetrated my face mask. There wasn't much left of the house. Or of its furnishings. Just blackened debris that someone would try to sort through later for any kind of salvageable photos and other valuables. Between the fire, smoke, and water damage from the firemen, there wouldn't be much to salvage.

There wasn't much to salvage from the two bodies, either. The larger one, assumed to be the husband, was propped against what was left of a wall. The other, presumably the wife, lay three feet away, next to a metal chair, her face burned beyond recognition.

"That poor child," Penelope had said in a rich Kentucky accent when she called me back as I drove toward the crime scene. "To be the center of so much gossip, and now this. Losing both of her parents." I imagined Penelope shaking her head and closing her eyes in prayer as she spoke to me. She was that type of woman— the praying type. I was glad she seemed to be on my side. I liked having that positive energy near me, even if I was incapable of returning it.

But it wasn't the seventeen-year-old girl I was thinking of now. My mind kept going to that awful night twelve years ago. I remembered that night like it was yesterday. It might as well have been yesterday with my screwed-up hyperthymesiac mind.

Too similar, I thought. The deaths. The fire. The positions of the bodies.

Chief Sam Reid sidled up beside me. His hair was thick and gray, and like me, he wore protective clothing to preserve the scene as much as possible. "The daughter hasn't been located yet," he said. Then, without giving me time to respond, he asked, "Does this look like a murder-suicide to you?"

I pushed my hair behind my ears and knelt down next to the wife's body while I pondered the chief's question. I snapped close-ups, then walked around to get different angles of the husband, the metal chair, and the rope again.

The chief was waiting patiently for my answer, so I stood and faced him. "Sir, I don't think I'm in a position—"

"Don't start with me, Faith," he interrupted. "You've been photographing and analyzing crime scenes long enough. You're like the nurse who knows more than the doctor. You run circles around my patrol officers, so until I hire another detective, you're the best I got to bounce theories off of." He crossed his arms and leaned into his heels, staring at me. Frustrated, he added, "Hell, you have a degree in forensic science and your uncle is the fire chief. Tell me what your gut is saying."

I removed my mask and breathed in the smoky air mixed with gasoline. "No, sir. I don't think this looks like a murder-suicide. I think it looks and smells like murder." I angled my head. "You think this has something to do with their daughter and the school teacher?"

"I suppose word of the arrest got around already." He rubbed fingers across his unshaven face.

"Chief, this *is* Paynes Creek."

The sound of a slamming car door had the chief and me turning toward the driveway. Paynes Creek Fire Chief Henry Nash stepped out of his vehicle. He paused to survey the damage before slipping into his own outerwear and footies.

"Have you heard from Ethan?" Chief Reid asked.

I jerked in his direction again. "Why do you ask?"

"Just wondering if he's made contact with any of you."

"He hasn't," I said simply. "Not with me."

The coroner's car and a white van arrived. A barricade was set up down the block, and several uniforms were stationed at the tape to keep people from coming too close to the crime scene, but it was near impossible to keep everyone away. A steady flow of residents huddled together in small packs across the street, sipping their morning coffee and shaking their heads.

Chief Nash ducked under the tape and walked cautiously over to where we stood. "Doesn't take a genius to determine this was arson, does it? This place reeks of gasoline." He looked at me. "You okay?"

I nodded. "Hi, Uncle Henry. I'm fine." I was sure he knew I was lying. I was certainly not okay. This crime scene hit too close to home.

Uncle Henry's thick golden hair and dark complexion always reminded me of my mother. He once told me that his nickname in high school had been "California." It was he and his wife who took me in after my mom died; I lived with them as I finished up my last year in high school. My brother had wanted to take care of me, but he was finishing up his undergraduate degree at the University of Kentucky and had just been admitted to Auburn University's veterinarian school. And everyone agreed it was best that he finish college and proceed straight to vet school. I knew everyone hoped I would be off to college in a year, I'd move on from the tragedy, and everything would be okay.

I did go off to college. The rest of the plan didn't go so well.

Chief Reid angled his head, studying me as if he'd only just now realized that this scene might be hard on me.

The squeal of tires pierced the crisp morning air, followed by a high-pitched scream. I spun to see Bella Reynolds getting out of a red sedan.

"Well, I guess we've found the daughter," Chief Reid said under his breath. "Who the hell let her through the barricade?"

The coroner was closest to her, and he stopped her from running through the red caution tape like she'd just finished first in a marathon. Unfortunately for her, I knew the marathon was yet to come. The longest race of her life would be trying to forget the image of the people she loved most being burned to a crisp. Even if she didn't actually see the bodies, her mind would conjure up the image—and it would haunt her forever.

She was still screaming hysterically, held by the coroner, as Chief Reid walked over to her. "What happened? Oh, God! Mom! Dad! Nooo!" Her screams turned into sobs.

It was yet another replay of a horrific moment I'd experienced myself.

As Chief Reid comforted the girl, I turned to Uncle Henry. "He thinks it's Ethan, doesn't he?"

"Ethan's name was mentioned when Sam called last night."

Ethan had been sentenced to life in prison, but in a shocking turn of events, he was released less than a month ago. He had put in a request for an appeal of his verdict, based on exculpatory evidence hidden from the public defender during the original trial. And it must have been quite the collection of evidence withheld, because not only was the appeal approved, but the commonwealth's attorney decided to drop all charges almost immediately thereafter. And then the judge did something completely unprecedented: he sealed the evidence and kept it from being released to the public.

Uncle Henry sighed. "When he was released, I knew his name would be thrown around in any arson investigations that came up. The public still believes he's guilty—there's no reason for them to think otherwise, since the evidence is sealed—and you know he's on the radar of reporters, too. They all want the story." He looked down at me. "Do you know where he went after his release?"

"Me? Why would I know?"

"The two of you were close once. I thought if he contacted anyone…"

My body tensed, and a wave of dread and nausea rose from my gut. I quickly changed the subject. "I've got enough photos," I said. "I'll have the station send copies to you."

I started to edge past my uncle, but he grabbed my arm and held firmly, forcing me to look him in the eye.

"You're not safe at the farm, Faith. I don't even care why the prosecutors decided to drop those charges—Ethan is still a dangerous man. And twelve years in the state pen can't have helped. We don't know what kind of person he is now."

"If Ethan means me harm, I'm not safe anywhere," I spat. I pulled my arm from my uncle's grasp. He liked to treat me like I was still a teenager, but I hadn't been a young girl in a very long time. I knew how to take care of myself. "He should never have been let out."

The way I saw it, Ethan's release was the fault of the fire and police investigators, who must have made some sort of procedural mistake. They should have made sure the evidence was tight all those years ago. But I couldn't say that to Uncle Henry, because he'd been involved in the investigation. Chief Reid, too. They'd spent a lot of hours collecting evidence and building a timeline that convinced both a jury and me that Ethan was guilty. Which only made me hate Ethan even more.

Bella still wailed. She was facing more heartache than a seventeen-year-old should have to face. Lucky for her, she'd only have to live through it once. I lived through it every single day of my life, reliving my most significant memories over and over again. And according to the slew of doctors and therapists I'd seen over the years, there wasn't a damn thing I could do about it.

An angry heat rose in my cheeks when I spotted a reporter snapping photos of the chief and Bella, forever preserving the girl's grief. I spun back to face Uncle Henry. "Instead of worrying about me, you ought to work on your barricades. Someone needs to keep those vultures out of your crime scene."

THE BACK ENTRANCE to Boone's Taphouse stank of stale beer kegs and rotten food at eight thirty in the morning. The restaurant and bar wouldn't open for another two and a half hours, but I knew Caine would be there. Sure enough, when I entered, I heard his deep voice yelling obscenities from the storeroom.

I pushed opened the door. He was leaning an elbow against a stack of boxes, his other hand was massaging his temple, and he was speaking loudly into his phone. His blond, shaggy hair was already a mess—he'd clearly been running his hand through it quite a bit. He spotted me, and I motioned that I would be at the bar.

The bar was mahogany-topped, with leather that was stained with rings and scratches, giving it a weathered look. I grabbed a glass, reached for a bottle of Caine's finest bourbon, and poured myself a finger's worth. I threw it back, marveling in its smooth, rich taste as it slid past my tongue and warmed my throat. Then I poured a couple more fingers.

"Help yourself," Caine said sarcastically as he joined me behind the bar.

"You were busy." I shrugged, then circled the bar and slid into a stool.

Caine grabbed himself a larger glass and fixed a soda. "Tough scene this morning?"

"House fire. Two people dead."

"I heard. You okay?"

I lifted the glass and nodded at it.

"Point taken." He pulled out a clipboard and began making checkmarks.

"Why haven't you married?" I asked him while swirling the amber liquid around in the tumbler.

Caine was a handsome man who'd just turned thirty. The regulars of Boone's Taphouse had thrown him a birthday party complete with a store-bought cake and tons of black balloons—which, of course, Caine had had to clean up afterward. He didn't seem to mind, though.

He cocked a single brow. "Is that a proposal?"

"Sure." I grinned. "Let's go down to the courthouse right now. Give old Mrs. Kenny a big surprise."

"You know I'm gay, right?" he asked in all seriousness.

I shrugged. "We'll never have to worry about breaking each other's hearts." I took another sip of bourbon. The visions of the two charred bodies had faded during the conversation, but they snapped back now, as did the memories of my own mother and her husband dying in similar fashion.

Over the years, I'd tried to learn how to hold back the flood of emotion I'd felt when my mother died, but nothing worked. I didn't need anything to trigger memories—they just happened—and every time, they were as fresh as they had been the moment they occurred. Not just the images, but the *feelings*. And I had to live with them forever.

Things would be better for Bella Reynolds. Her memories would fade and evolve. She would replace the worst memories with happier ones, and eventually she would heal and move on with her life, while keeping fond memories of certain parts of her childhood. Only occasionally would she have to shove those terrible memories back inside their box.

I felt a sudden, ugly wave of envy. There were no lids to my memory boxes.

My phone buzzed in my back pocket, and I pulled it out. "Faith Day," I said.

"Hi, Faith. It's Penelope. Chief wants to see you." She lowered her voice. "We've got ourselves a fed in here."

What the hell was a fed doing in Paynes Creek? "Okay. I'll be right there." I hung up and drained the rest of my bourbon. "Duty calls, Caine. Thanks for the drink."

"Why do you stay with that horrible job?" Caine asked. "Why would you want to photograph death and destruction for a living?"

I forced a smile. "Why do you listen to everyone's sob

stories at the bar day after day? Doesn't that bring you down?"

"I'd like to think I'm helping. Giving them an ear that they can't get elsewhere."

"Well, maybe I think that by photographing crime scenes, I'm giving victims a voice they no longer have."

That sounded pretty good. Even though it was a lie.

That night twelve years ago was not the only horrifying memory I had to live with. And with every crime scene I photographed, I hoped to form memories that might, somehow, replace those of my past—the ones I kept secret *and* the ones that made me a liar.

THREE

While driving to the Paynes Creek Police Department, I sucked on six Altoids. It was highly unlikely anyone would get close enough to me to smell the bourbon on my breath, but it was still a good precaution.

Besides, I wasn't an on-duty police officer. I was a contractor. When there was a crime scene or car accident to be photographed, the police called me, but beyond that, my time was my own. Yes, I was basically always on call—crimes and accidents didn't confine themselves to the convenient hours between eight and five—but I could have a drink when I wanted to have a drink. No one controlled me.

That's what I told myself, anyway.

The police station was buzzing. A couple of the more seasoned officers were chatting in the corner to my right when I pushed through the double glass doors. They straightened and stared at me when I entered, then I heard one of them—red-headed and freckled—mutter, "Did you hear that she called about an intruder in her house last week? When officers got there, they didn't find shit."

"Crazy bitch," the other one said. "To think I fell for that dare to ask her out when I first started."

"We all do," Red said, laughing. "She never says yes."

Penelope sat at her desk with a Bluetooth headset connected to her ear. She looked up when I approached. "Hi, honey!" She chomped gum like a teenager and fiddled with the cross around her neck. Then she leaned across the desk and motioned with her finger for me to come closer. "Wait 'til you see the yumminess in the chief's office." She cast a mischievous look toward Chief Reid's office before sitting back with a wide grin.

I lifted a brow. "Penelope, you might need to lay off the coffee."

She rolled her eyes. "I'm just thinking of you. Go in there and be real nice, and you just might get to give him the grand tour of Paynes Creek."

If I was the type to roll my eyes, I would have done it then. Penelope was always either trying to marry me off or trying to get me into a church pew every Sunday. It would have irritated me except that I tried not to ever be angry with Penelope. She was the buffer between Chief Reid and me, and she kept me informed of all the gossip—especially the gossip concerning me.

She hadn't changed much since we'd attended Paynes Creek High School together. We weren't friends back then, but I always knew who she was. She was popular—hung out with the cheerleader crowd even though she wasn't a cheerleader. The guys listened to her, but didn't really date her. She was everyone's best friend and was known for helping everyone with their problems.

And just as she had handled her friends' issues in high school, she now handled—or mothered—the patrol officers she worked with. She brought in food and consoled them after bad days. She was a good wife to an EMT who often worked the night shift, and she was an amazing mother to a three-year-old boy. She had a great big ol' heart, and I always thought of her when I heard a southerner say, "Bless her heart. She means well."

"Faith," Chief called from the doorway of his office. I flinched, causing Penelope to narrow her eyes at me. "Can you come here?"

Penelope pretended to tidy papers on her desk as she mouthed the words *Be nice*. She had a look on her face as if I'd just been summoned to the principal's office and she couldn't wait to hear the details when I got out. With her curly red hair teased into a clip on the back of her head, even her appearance reminded me of high school.

My black combat boots squeaked against the tile as I walked over to the chief's office. One of the newer patrol officers looked up from his desk as I passed, but immediately averted his eyes. The younger cops were frightened of me. They'd heard the stories of what I'd been through, and were terrified to get into a conversation with me for fear I might finally snap. That didn't bother me. I wasn't much for chitchat.

I stepped into the chief's office. He was seated on the other side of his desk, and another man sat in one of the guest chairs. So this was the fed. He was in his low- to mid-thirties, dark-haired, and wore a navy blue suit. The suit was typical of FBI agents, but the tie was pink and featured... were those giraffes?

"Faith, I want you to meet Special Agent Luke Justice. Agent, Faith Day."

Special Agent Justice stood and held out his hand. "Luke," he said in a smooth voice. He commanded the room with his large, muscular presence. When I got a closer look, I saw that his suit wasn't so typical—it was made of a beautiful, rich fabric. And the pink giraffe tie was silk. "I hear you're the station's forensic photographer."

I gave him my hand, and he squeezed it firmly while making eye contact with me. "I'm a forensic photographer, yes. I work on a contract basis." I hated how Chief Reid was always telling people I worked for the station like I was an employee he owned. I was my own boss, and I preferred to make that clear.

I knew almost immediately that Special Agent Justice was the kind of man who could read you with a simple look—and he was giving me that look now. I made a mental note to stay clear of him.

"Faith, Special Agent Justice is here to help us on the Reynolds case."

"Okay," I said. Why was he telling me? I had nothing to do with the investigation other than taking the photos. And why was this a federal case? "You want me to make sure Special Agent Justice receives a copy of the photos?"

Instead of Chief answering, Luke said, "Miss Day, I'm investigating a string of fires."

I eyed him. My palms began to sweat, and I resisted the urge to wipe them on my pants. "A string of fires," I repeated.

"Yes."

I looked to the chief and back to Luke. "You mean, like a serial arsonist?"

He shifted. "Possibly. However, serial arsonists typically take a cooling-off period between fires, and the fires in recent weeks have been rather close together. So I'm looking at a lot of possibilities."

"And you think last night's fire fits into the series you're investigating."

"Maybe."

His one-word answer irritated me. "What do you need from me, Agent?"

"Are you aware that Ethan Gentry was released from prison less than three weeks ago?"

"Yes," I said simply.

"He's your brother, right?"

"Stepbrother."

"Has he contacted you?"

"No." Visions of my stepbrother—not what he looked like now, but how he looked, sounded, even smelled twelve years ago—poured into my head.

"I'm told you had an incident on your property a few nights ago."

I glanced uneasily at Chief Reid, then back at the agent. "At three seventeen a.m. Sunday."

I saw no reason to hide anything now—I'd already reported the incident. I thought of the daisies that had been left on my bed and of the fire in my fire pit. I also thought of the fire on my property this morning and the candles that were lit inside. I had no proof that Ethan had come into my trailer or set those fires, but it hadn't escaped my imagination that he might reach out to me in some way.

Nor had he escaped the FBI's radar, it would seem.

"Faith," Chief said, shifting on his feet. Chief Reid was one of the people who had dismissed my incident report last week as either a cry for attention or a prank by some local kids. "Agent Justice is here to investigate the fire that happened last night. If you could—"

"I'll give him a copy of every photograph I took and cooperate in any way I can." I shifted my gaze to Luke. "If the two of you will excuse me, I'm expected in court." I turned on my heel and exited Chief's office before either of them could stop me.

I walked as naturally as I could manage toward the exit of the police station, but once I was outside, I ran. I took a hard left at the corner and sped down an alleyway that opened up into a parking lot behind the buildings. Spotting a dumpster, I ducked behind it and promptly threw up my breakfast of champions. The bourbon had sure felt better on the way down than it did coming back up.

This could not be happening. I would *not* let them bring Ethan back into my life. He was a part of my past, and I wanted to keep him there. I would not give Ethan any power in my life. And suddenly I felt certain it was Ethan who had been lighting fires and candles on my property. The next time he showed up, I'd be ready for him.

WHEN I WAS sure I wouldn't be sick again, I emerged from behind the dumpster, only to find a woman standing beside a news van nearby. She and a cameraman walked quickly toward me.

"Faith? Faith Day?"

I turned and walked away, not even acknowledging that she had the right person.

"Faith. It's me, Marla Manfield."

I paused. Turned slowly toward her. Her hair was as red and dark as chili powder, styled in a perfect and smooth bob. She wore dark rose lipstick and thick brown eyeshadow on lids decorated with even thicker fake eyelashes. Marla Manfield had graduated from Paynes Creek the same year as my brother Finch—four years before me. She'd been captain of the cheerleading squad, had dated the most popular football player, and had gotten out of two DUIs the year after graduation thanks to a father who was a golf buddy of the commonwealth's attorney. There were perks to growing up popular and wealthy in Paynes Creek. Or there had been, back then. In recent years, the good ol' boy system had suffered some cracks, and it was no longer nearly as easy to get a lesser punishment on a repeat DUI charge.

Not that Marla would need that kind of help now. She had cleaned up her act, becoming a news reporter for one of the local networks in Lexington, and from what I'd seen, she'd made her mark in sensationalist reporting. Always going after the difficult stories even if it meant embellishing the details.

I realized I was staring at her. She hadn't spoken other than to announce her name in case I didn't recognize her. But I did recognize her. I even remembered what she wore the one and only time she went out with Finch. My condition allowed me to remember the tiniest and most inconsequential of details, yet I couldn't remember why they'd had only one date that summer after their sophomore year in college. I guess I never knew. Maybe Finch had already met Aubrey, his now wife? Regardless, I saw the two of them at a party that summer night. Mom and Eli—Ethan's dad—had said that at sixteen, I was too young to go to a field party with my friends, but when Ethan offered to go with me, they said it was okay. The double standard had made me mad. Ethan was only sixteen then, too, yet they trusted him with my safety.

Hell, back then I trusted him too.

"I'd like to say you haven't changed a bit, but look at you," she said, giving me a once-over. "You're beautiful. You always were pretty, but now you're even more stunning."

I angled my head and studied the way her eyeliner perfectly lined the lid and curved up at the edges. My hand went instinctively to my neck where I knew burn scars crept up toward my face. Was that really how she got people to talk to her? Pay them some empty compliment? I let my eyes drift to the videographer standing just over her right shoulder. He had the decency to look embarrassed. And he had yet to point his camera at me, or I wouldn't still be standing there.

"Do you mind if I ask you some questions?" Marla asked.

"As a matter of fact," I started, but then curiosity got the better of me. "About what?"

"Your brother."

Last night's fire, the arrest of a school teacher, Ethan getting out of prison... All of those possibilities had run through my mind, but not Finch. "Finch? What about him?" If she wanted information about Finch, why not go to Finch?

"Right." She looked away for a second. "I meant Ethan."

A pregnant pause stretched between us. "Ethan is not my brother." I shifted from one foot to the other, my eyes glued to hers. "I have nothing to say about him."

"So you don't care that they're speculating he might be starting fires again now that he's out?"

"Who is they?" I asked. "I haven't heard anyone say that." The accusation didn't surprise me; I had known it was only a matter of time. And news crews from across the region had already begun flocking to Paynes Creek to report on the schoolteacher incident. The media just loves a salacious teacher-student story. Now they would be on hand to report on something almost as sexy: a murder-suicide topped with arson. And they'd all be looking for fresh angles—like connecting this morning's crime to Ethan's recent release. Even if they had to manufacture that connection.

Marla smiled. It was creepy how she tried to come across as a friend in order to get information. "Sources who shall remain nameless for now."

"You have nothing." I turned and started away from her.

"I talked to Ethan," she said quickly. "He's claiming you knew he didn't start the fire that killed your parents. And he says he has proof."

That made me pause. But I knew better than to engage with a bloodsucking sensationalist, so I kept walking.

FOUR

My Airstream was perched on land that Finch and I —and technically Ethan—had inherited from my mom and stepfather. Finch wanted nothing to do with the land, and Ethan had been sent to prison, so it had effectively been left to me. I decided that if I was going to have to relive the memories of what happened to me every day of my life, I might as well do it on beautiful, coveted farmland in a familiar town. And as I didn't require much space —or the money to rebuild the house—the Airstream became my home. Mine and Gus's.

I had gutted and remodeled the inside of the trailer, reconstructing it for efficiency and comfort. If I ever decided I'd had enough of Paynes Creek, I could hitch my home to the back of my SUV and be in another town in less than a day. But I liked this farm in the middle of Kentucky's thoroughbred horse country. It was where I had grown up. And though I had bad memories here— worse memories than most people accumulated in a lifetime—I had good ones, too. This was where my mother

27

gave Finch and me the best years of our lives, before our father died of cancer when I was ten. I liked to think that the spirits of both my parents were still on this farm, protecting me.

Of course, I knew that was stupid. My father's spirit certainly never protected me from what happened after Ethan and his father moved in.

As I walked into my trailer and threw my keys on the kitchen counter, I looked out the window toward the woods. A walking path led through the trees to the creek that marked the boundary between my property and the neighboring farm, which was recently purchased by a Paynes Creek prodigal son—former FBI Special Agent Cooper Adams. The gossip hens hadn't let up about that one; reportedly he'd left the FBI after a case went "terribly wrong." No one had any real details, but that didn't stop them from talking about it.

I felt sorry for the man. He was one of the successful few who'd made it out of Paynes Creek to do good in the world... and now he was not only back, but the subject of gossip. I felt strongly that a man had the right to keep his story to himself for however long he needed.

But I did wonder about one thing: I wondered if Cooper and Luke knew each other.

Luke. I sighed, and not in a good way. It sure hadn't taken long for him to start asking questions about Ethan. Did the FBI really believe Ethan had earned his freedom from incarceration only to start setting fires again?

Gus staggered in from the bedroom. When I wasn't here, she always seemed to find her way into my bed.

"Hey, girl!" I scratched behind her ears. She leaned into the touch, then headed for the door. "You want to go out?" I pushed open the door and let her out. I loved that she preferred to use the bathroom outside the trailer, even though she had a litter box tucked inside a cabinet with a small pet door.

Following Gus outside and to the back of the trailer, I stared at the foundation where my childhood home had once stood. I could still see the out-of-control flames and smell the billowing smoke from that night. I could still hear what I thought were my mom's and Eli's screams just as I arrived—even though I was later told that there was no way I heard their screams because they were killed prior to the fire being set. My hand went instinctively to my throat and neck where flames had scarred my skin; I could still feel the heat as I ran in, screaming, in an attempt to save my mother. I couldn't forget a single aspect of that night, even after all these years—and seeing Bella this morning had only heightened my anguish.

Gus completed her business, ran past me toward the fire pit, and began to sniff around the logs. Sometimes she acted more like a dog than a cat.

A shiver moved down my spine as I remembered the figure standing there this morning. That was different —bolder.

Gus batted at something in the grass.

"You find something, girl?"

I searched the area she was sniffing. "There's nothing th—" But then I saw it. Beside one of the logs was a matchbook. I picked it up and turned it over in my fingers. *The Spotted Cat*, it read. The Spotted Cat was a music club in Lexington that featured local bands and musicians. The name and idea behind the club came from a hot jazz spot in New Orleans. I remembered reading about how it was opened by a New Orleans native who'd relocated to Lexington, though I was pretty sure it had changed owner-ship recently.

Gus lost interest and took off toward the Airstream. I

followed her in and poured myself a stiff glass of bourbon over ice. Then I went to my closet and pulled an oversized photo box from a hidden compartment beneath the floor of the closet. I put it on my bed, set the lid to one side, and, with my bourbon in one hand, began pulling things out.

On top were a few childhood pictures of me and Finch, given to me by Aunt Leah. Beneath that was some journals I kept at the suggestion of a therapist I'd begun seeing while I was in high school. And underneath those were the crime scene photos from the night my childhood ended.

I shouldn't even have these. I came across them at Uncle Henry's house one day while I was home from college, and I stole them. I told myself he probably shouldn't have kept a copy either, even though he was the fire chief and had more official right to them than I did.

Crime scene photos always told a story. They told the truth of what happened, even when the victims were no longer around to reveal the details.

I took a sip of bourbon, relishing the rich warmth of the liquor. Then I spread the photos in a grid so that I could take them in. Why I felt the need to do this, I wasn't sure. I had committed every photo to memory twelve years ago, and I'd studied them again recently when I learned Ethan had a good chance of being released on appeal. But what I hadn't done either of those times was figure out the story hidden in the pictures. I knew it was a sad story—that much was for certain. Heart-wrenching. But parts of the story were missing. And those missing elements weren't inside my memories.

Most importantly, I never saw who killed my mom and Eli. I never knew the truth. But *someone* did. And if Ethan really was innocent, that someone had to be feeling nervous as a cat right now.

FIVE

The funeral for Sandra and Gordon Reynolds took place on a Monday. It was a cold, dark, and dreary day, but the town showed up in a big way, as close-knit southern communities are prone to do. The church was filled with family and friends, including friends of Bella's—and what space was left over was taken up by nosy neighbors and people who just wanted to gawk at the latest scandal. There was no graveside service, since the bodies remained in the hands of the coroner—and there wouldn't be much to bury when the bodies were released anyway. If it were me, I'd go ahead and request a cremation once cause of death was officially determined.

The wake was held at the house of Janice Jones, Sandra Reynolds's younger sister, with the help of ladies from the church, of course. She had also insisted on taking Bella in; Janice wasn't married and didn't have children of her own. In fact she was heavily gossiped about around town because she partied hard most weekend nights and was stuck in a desperate search for a husband with a revolving door of suitors. Paynes Creek was a tough place to be a single woman past her teenage years—most bachelors in their thirties carried too much baggage to bother with. You had to give Janice credit for not giving up.

Currently she was circling the room, placing coasters underneath drinks in order to protect her inexpensive, bulk-made furniture, carrying abandoned plates of food back to the kitchen, and generally staying busy. Her blond hair was long and had been hot-rollered into loose spirals, but her eyes were bloodshot, and I noticed that people had been watching her with increased interest as the day wore on.

"Did you hear?" I overheard a woman say behind me. I turned and saw that she was huddled with another woman. "Sandra and Gordon invited Mr. Lake into their home for dinner and drinks quite often. Talk about letting the wolf guard the henhouse." The woman talking wore a black dress that hung past her knees, and a scarf that reminded me of a peacock was wrapped around her neck and shoulder.

The other woman held a glass of clear liquid up next to her mouth as if to keep others from hearing her. "I heard he passed out on their sofa one night." She was dressed in black pants and a gray sweater. A string of pearls decorated her neck. "I don't see how Sandra *or* Gordon couldn't have known that something was going on with their daughter and Mr. Lake. My son says everyone at school knew, and had known for months."

Miss Peacock and Miss Pearls nodded in agreement of each other as if they'd just solved all the town's problems and its latest crime.

"Well, that teacher is only twenty-four," Miss Peacock said. "He's not even that much older than Bella."

I lifted a brow. Was the woman seriously suggesting

that it was okay for a twenty-four-year-old teacher to have relations with a seventeen-year-old student?

"Oh, Darlene," Miss Pearls said with a chuckle. "You know that doesn't make it right. He was in a position of authority." She sounded like she was quoting a newspaper article.

The two women were just a couple of gossips, but they did make me wonder if Bella's parents had known about Mr. Lake and their daughter. And whether they'd been in favor of him being arrested.

"The Reynoldses sure were popular," a male voice said behind me.

Startled, I tensed, turned, and stared into the moss-green eyes of Special Agent Luke Justice. He was probably here to see if the person who burned down the Reynoldses' home would show up at the funeral. That was a typical line of thought for investigators of serious crimes.

He scanned the room over my head. "Were all of these people their friends?"

I looked over my shoulder, then turned back to him and lifted a plastic cup filled with cheap white wine to my lips. After swallowing the really bad wine, I met his gaze and said, "No. No one is *this* popular in this town. But welcome to Paynes Creek, where everyone pretends to be your friend until they don't."

"What does that mean?"

"Stick around a while, Agent. You'll figure it out."

A loud commotion erupted outside in front of the house. I slipped through the crowd and out the front door to see what was happening. Luke was on my heels.

Bella Reynolds was standing on the sidewalk, practically screaming at her aunt, her high-pitched southern accent piercing the air. "You will *never* be my mother! My real mama and daddy are dead!"

I couldn't help but feel sorry for her, even though she sounded like a spoiled brat at the moment. She was entitled to her grief.

"They no longer have any say in who I see or where I go," Bella continued. "And neither do you!" She turned and headed for a cheap sedan that appeared to be waiting for her.

Someone approached Janice from behind and whispered something in her ear that I imagined went along the lines of, *Let her go. She's mourning. She'll be back.*

As Bella climbed into the car, Luke muttered beside me, "Matthew Lake, you are one stupid son of a bitch." I didn't get a good look at the man in the car, but Luke seemed pretty confident it was the high school teacher. I knew he wasn't still in custody—he had been released when the prosecuting attorney decided she didn't have enough evidence that he and Bella had actually engaged in sex. And Bella denied it vehemently—claimed her teacher had only been giving her private violin lessons leading up to an audition.

"Bella! You can't leave!" Janice screamed, running after the car.

Bella just tossed a wave out the car window as it sped off.

As one car left, another arrived. My brother, Finch Day, the beloved town veterinarian, had decided to make a late appearance. He got out the driver's side and was most of the way around to help his wife, Aubrey, from the car, when a reporter jumped in front of him. The woman snapped his photo, then stuck out a hand holding a phone, which I assumed was set to record.

"Mr. Day, do you believe your stepbrother set the fire that killed Sandra and Gordon Reynolds? Have you heard from Ethan Gentry since he was released from prison?"

Where I would have shoved the leech out of the way and ordered her to leave, Finch merely squared his shoulders. "I do not know if Ethan set the fire. I'll leave that to investigators to figure out." He cast a glance in my direction, then returned his attention to the reporter. "No, I have not heard from him. And you need to leave. This is highly inappropriate, and if you had any decency, you would know that already."

He nudged past the reporter and joined his wife, who had stepped from the car holding a plate of deviled eggs covered in Saran Wrap—a funeral staple here in the south. She made eye contact with me as well.

I spun around with the intention of finding my way to my car and leaving, but I was blocked by Agent Justice. I attempted to get around him, but he stopped me with a hand on my forearm.

"Where's the fire?" He closed his eyes. "Sorry. Bad choice of words."

"Let me pass."

He looked over my shoulder, then back at me. I don't know what he saw in my expression, but his eyes softened. "Let's get out of here."

I had no intention of leaving with him, but I did let him lead me away. Behind me, I heard several people shouting hello to Finch—or "Doc," as everyone called him —and I hoped they would corral him and Aubrey and allow me to make my escape.

No such luck.

"Faith."

I stopped, closed my eyes for moment, then turned to face my brother. "Hi, Finch. Aubrey."

"Hey, Faith. You doing okay?" Aubrey spoke with a thick, Louisiana drawl. Her family was from New Orleans —fourth-generation Creole.

"I'm fine, thanks. How are you doing? Feeling alright?" I glanced down at her gently swollen belly.

"I'm hanging in there." She rubbed her belly. She was starting to show, and because it was their first, they didn't even try to hide their excitement. "I'm just sick about what happened to the Reynoldses, though. First their daughter is assaulted by that poor excuse for a teacher, and now her parents are dead. That poor child." She looked down at her protruding stomach. "I'll never let anything like this happen to you, sweetie." She looked back up at me and smiled. "The books say your baby can hear you speaking to them from real early on." Leaving her hand on her stomach like a protective shield, she nodded toward Luke. "Who's your friend?"

"Oh." I looked at Luke. "He's not my friend. Special Agent Luke Justice, Finch and Aubrey Day."

Finch stepped forward and held out his hand. "Special Agent. As in FBI?" he asked.

"That's right. I'm investigating a series of deadly fires, including the one that killed the Reynoldses." I noticed that he lowered his voice. At least he had the decency to know how to behave at a funeral.

But Aubrey's ears seemed to perk up. "Oh! You think someone burned the Reynoldses' home on purpose?"

"We're looking at all angles," Luke said.

Typical investigator response.

"Did you photograph the crime scene?" Finch asked me.

"That's my job."

Finch shifted from foot to foot. "Can I talk to you a second? In private?"

"Can we do it later? I was just on my way out."

"And we need to pay our respects," Aubrey said, saving me.

"Then can I call you later?" Finch asked. "We really need to talk."

"Sure."

Aubrey was pulling on his arm. "I'll call you later, too, Faith." She gave me a quick wink and a smile over her shoulder as she urged Finch to come with her. "And nice to meet you, Mr. Justice."

I'd nearly forgotten that Luke was still standing there.

"That's the local veterinarian, right?" he said. "And he's your brother? I get the sense that he's respected in the community."

I stared straight into his eyes. "If you're looking for information, Special Agent, you're going to have to stop sounding like an interrogator. Now if you'll excuse me, I need a real drink."

BOONE'S TAPHOUSE was just gearing up for the dinner crowd when I entered, so it wasn't that crowded. I immediately spotted Matthew Lake and Bella Reynolds tucked into a booth in the back, sitting side by side. Across the table from them were two girls I didn't know, but who looked like high school students.

I slid into a seat at the bar. Caine approached with a glass and a bottle of Kentucky bourbon—Elkhorn Reserve. It was a favorite in the area. "You go to the funeral?" he asked while pouring.

"Yeah. They had a church service and a wake at Janice Jones's house." As I took a sip, I swiveled in the stool to study Matthew and the three girls in the back booth. "What do you make of that?" I asked.

"They're not breaking the law by being in my establishment, so I'm trying to stay out of it. But I'm afraid as soon as the wrong person walks in, all hell will break loose. Then I'm going to care. A lot!"

I turned back to Caine. "And the last thing Matthew needs is to be the center of a bar brawl. Or he'll find himself right back in jail."

"Hey," Caine chastised. "This is not a bar. This is a fine dining establishment."

"With a bar," I said. "And if a fight breaks out, you've got yourself a brawl. And a reputation. It takes far less than what's going on in that booth to get this town chattering."

"And hopefully far more than that to ruin the reputation of my restaurant, because don't look now, but the fed just walked in. That's something else people are yammering about."

I looked toward the door and saw Luke chatting it up with the hostess. "How did you know he was a fed?" I asked. But the answer was obvious. Luke's entire look screamed FBI. He wore a dark suit, a tie loosened at the neck, and his hair was disheveled, like someone who had just had sex or had worked a long, trying day. Since I knew he had just come from a funeral, I decided on the latter.

"He came in for lunch. I spotted that tall drink of sweet tea immediately," Caine said.

I noted that the hostess now had a hand on Luke's forearm. "Looks like you're not the only one who spotted him." I turned back to Caine with a lifted brow, unable to contain a slight annoyance at Luke's easy way with another woman.

"So tell me," Caine said, bringing the conversation back between us, "is it true that Bella's parents knew about her relationship with the teacher?"

I shrugged. "If you believe the rumors."

Caine's eyes lifted to someone behind me. "What can I get you?" he asked.

Luke slid onto a stool beside mine. He looked over at my glass, and with no originality whatsoever, said, "I'll have what she's having."

Caine poured Luke a glass, then tipped the bottle in my direction. I nodded, and he gave me another pour. He then went off to tend to other customers.

"I figured since you were going for a real drink, I'd find you here." Luke faced forward, sipping his bourbon.

"You come to have a drink with me, Agent? Or did you come to question me some more?"

He turned, and I could feel him analyzing my profile. "You're an interesting woman, Faith."

I shot a lazy look his way. "And what, exactly, makes you the authority on that?"

"I have eyes and ears. When you walk through a room, people watch you. When you exit a room, people whisper. And when you exit a building, people sigh with relief."

My lips curved upward. "Really? You got all that after just a few days of being here?"

He faced forward again. "If you don't want to talk about yourself, tell me about your brother. Or we can discuss your stepbrother."

"So this *is* an interview," I said.

He motioned for Caine to pour him more bourbon. Took a sip when he had. Facing me, he said, "I'm not just investigating the recent string of fires. I'm also looking into the facts surrounding the fire that killed your mother and her husband."

My grip around my glass tightened. "It's been twelve years. Are they reopening the case?" I asked so softly I almost didn't hear my own voice.

A more important question was: Did the state truly

believe Ethan was innocent? The commonwealth's attorney had decided not to retry him for murder, but without knowing the evidence that had prompted that decision, I couldn't say whether it was truly exculpatory or merely driven by a procedural issue. Uncle Henry had told me that a witness had come forward with proof that the prosecutor's timeline for that night was severely flawed—but that wasn't necessarily proof of innocence.

"Not exactly."

I drained my glass of bourbon, then stood. "If you truly heard what people said when I left rooms and buildings, you'd know that I don't appreciate people prying into my life uninvited. You'd also know that most men would warn you to stay away from me, as I tend to bring trouble everywhere I go." I stepped close to him and placed a palm against his face. "And here I thought I was going to like you."

"There's a lot to like," he said, his eyes glued to mine. "I think if you gave me a chance… got to know me…"

What I did next was completely out of character. Maybe it was because it had been a long time since I'd been with a man. Maybe it was because I liked the way he flirted and I knew he was blowing in and out of town so fast that his presence wouldn't last. Maybe it was because I just fucking wanted to embrace the opportunity. But I smiled, leaned in, and touched my lips to his.

I'd wondered what his lips would feel like when I was at the wake, but never did I imagine I'd actually feel them so soon.

They were soft. And he was gentle. Until I felt a slight shift—quick, like a lightning reflex—and he slid a hand to the back of my neck, stood, and deepened the kiss.

When I pulled away, I kept my lips close to his. "Stay away from me. Stay away from my brother."

He smiled. "I don't think I can."

"Try."

BELLA AND MATTHEW were in the parking lot when I exited Boone's, and they appeared to be arguing.

I took my time walking to my SUV, wanting to see if Bella needed help.

"Did you promise her my scholarship?" Bella screamed at Matthew.

"Of course not," he answered.

Was Matthew helping Bella get a college scholarship? I imagined her parents might have been thrilled about that. Maybe that was why they'd had him over to their house.

"Babe," he said, "you know I only have feelings for you."

I had been just about to open my car door, but when I heard this declaration, I paused and risked a glance in their direction.

Bella leaned her forehead into his chest. "I know. I'm sorry. I know you love me. But I have nothing now. Without that scholarship I'll never get out of this shithole town."

Her parents had been dead only a few days, and she was worried about some scholarship?

Matthew rested his chin on top of her head. I saw the moment of recognition when his eyes rose and found mine... when he realized they were speaking in a public parking lot. He slowly pushed Bella back. "Let's get you home. Your aunt will be worried."

Bella's head tilted backward. She seemed to read his face, then followed his gaze until she, too, was looking at me. Her face registered recognition, and her jaw hardened.

She marched toward me in quick, long strides. "You! This is your fault. People say you should have seen your brother start that fire—that your word would have kept him behind bars for life. Because he's out, my parents are dead!"

That verified that people were, in fact, linking Ethan to the recent fire.

I hadn't seen Luke exit Boone's, but suddenly he was beside me. "Miss Reynolds, I don't think this is the time or place to attack someone for something you know nothing about."

"Who the fuck are you?" she screamed, and I had to remind myself that she was a grieving seventeen-year-old kid.

"Special Agent Luke Justice—FBI."

"Justice?" She laughed. "What kind of name is that? Like I expect a worthless cop like you to get *me* justice."

Matthew had enough sense to back slowly away. Bella Reynolds really was an arrogant and angry teenager.

"Mr. Lake," said Luke, "I think it's time you get Miss Reynolds to her aunt's house. And if I were you, I'd stay clear of each other, or you're going to find yourself right back in jail."

"Oh, didn't you hear?" Bella said. "They're not gonna let Matthew be a teacher anymore. Because of dicks like you, he's got to find a new job."

I wasn't sure if she was calling him a dick because it was slang for cop, or if she was simply calling him a derogatory name. Probably both.

"He doesn't even get a trial. And we didn't do anything," Bella continued. "*You're* the one who should be put on trial." She was yelling at me again, and it was taking everything in me not to slap sense into her. "You lied, and now your brother is out, and he's killing people again."

"Okay... Let's go." Matthew physically turned Bella

and pulled her toward his car. When he had her settled in the passenger seat, he gave us a low wave. "Sorry. She's just upset about her parents. I'm taking her to her aunt's now."

When Matthew pulled out of the parking lot, Luke asked, "You alright?"

"I'm fine."

I turned back toward my car, but Luke pushed his way between me and the open door.

"You okay to drive?"

"I said I was fine." I stood there, letting his eyes burn into mine.

He seemed on the verge of asking me another question, but thought better of it. Stepping aside, he watched me slide behind the wheel and shut the door. Instead of taking a moment to catch my breath, I turned the ignition and drove out of that parking lot without looking back.

SIX

The next night, with the Spotted Cat matchbook sitting in the cup holder beside me, I turned my vehicle into the quaint, bordering on seedy, lounge. It was nestled beside a budget motel just across the county line from Paynes Creek. I parked, hopped out, and strode inside.

The place was dim, and a terrible five-piece jazz band played in one corner. One look at the trumpet player—an overweight, red-faced man dressed in a football jersey two sizes too small—made me worry he might keel over if he blew too hard. I hoped he didn't; I wasn't sure I had the mental capacity to perform CPR tonight.

I walked along the edges of the room, scanning the faces of the people sitting at the small round tables, looking for anyone familiar. I then made my way toward the bar, where a couple of men sat with two stools between them. Travelers, maybe. I figured there were two kinds of people at the Spotted Cat: tourists and regulars. This wasn't the type of establishment that drew new locals in on a daily or even a weekly basis. It was the same people night after night, plus those staying at the motel next door.

Which made me wonder how a matchbook with the Spotted Cat logo had landed near my fire pit. Was it simply that the lounge was situated close to Paynes Creek? Maybe Finch or Uncle Henry had been in here and had dropped the matchbook the last time the family gathered around the fire pit.

A couple of waitresses walked between the tables carrying trays of drinks. I noted that all the servers were female, and they wore short black dresses with white aprons—like something right out of the seventies. Such a getup took the women's movement back forty years.

I walked to the other end of the bar, as far away from the door as I could, and sat at a corner table that would allow me to see the door and the entire room. A waitress brought me a glass of water, and I ordered a glass of red wine.

And I waited.

For what, I wasn't sure. But since Paynes Creek PD hadn't taken the fire and break-in at my property seriously, I would.

The band played a couple more songs, then took a break.

As I sipped the house wine, which wasn't terrible, I twirled the matchbook in my fingers and studied the faces of the few people who entered. But by the time I'd drained my wine glass, I'd decided what I was doing was stupid. What did I think I was going to find? An arsonist? Someone easily recognized as a stalker, who had broken into my trailer while I was sleeping, lit some candles, then built a large bonfire? Would I know the person?

I pulled a ten from my pocket and set it under my glass. I was about to stand when I saw him.

He strolled into the lounge and walked right up to the bar like he owned the place. But he didn't stop there or grab a stool. He lifted a section of the hinged wooden bar top, ducked behind the bar, and started tying an apron around his waist.

Ethan is working at the Spotted Cat?

I sank lower in my seat, wishing I could somehow disappear. My heart thumped so hard in my chest that I placed a hand there to hold it in. I became lightheaded, and a ringing erupted in my ears so loud I thought I might pass out.

I could almost smell him—how I remembered him. Not the smell of cheap cologne that he wore when he went to school or out with friends or other girls, but the smell of soap and fresh country-living air—the way he smelled when he hung out with me at home, playing video games or doing the chores Mom and Eli assigned us.

I took a deep breath and focused on the napkin in front of me. A drop of red wine had created a splotch that looked like a watercolor painting. Another deep breath, and the volume of the ringing lowered slightly. Another, and my heart slowed a little.

When I had calmed enough, I looked up again. There was no way for me to exit the lounge without walking the entire length of the bar. He would see me for sure.

My waitress returned, blocking my view of the bar and of Ethan. "Can I get you anything else, hon?" She was chomping on a piece of gum. Her hair, the color of onyx, was piled high on top of her head in a messy bun. She was probably in her late twenties, though she was aging prematurely; the lines around her eyes and lips told me she was probably a smoker.

When she shifted from one foot to the other, I moved

with her, using her as a shield to keep from being seen by Ethan.

"Uh… yes," I said without really thinking about it, but then I reached a hand to her arm. She tensed. Her wide eyes looked from mine to the hand on her arm. I pulled it back. "Sorry. Is there a back way out of here?"

"Is everything okay, hon? You don't look so good."

"I just need to leave. And I don't want someone to see me."

"Okaaay," she said, long and drawn out. "Sure. There's a back door. Right through there." She stepped backwards and pointed with a full, outstretched arm at a door right next to the bar. But her movement left me exposed, and drew Ethan's attention.

He was putting the finishing touches on a dry martini at the end of the bar closest to us, but now he looked up, and our eyes met.

I froze. My breath was knocked out of me with that casual glance in my direction.

As recognition passed through his eyes and over his face, his entire body reacted. He quickly passed the drink across the bar to a customer, then wiped his hands on an apron around his waist.

I took the opportunity to dart from my chair. I ran the length of the bar toward the main exit.

"Faith?"

I heard him call out, but I didn't stop.

I pushed through the heavy wooden doors and ran straight into a bear of a man. "Oh, sorry," I said instinctively.

The man grabbed my arms to steady me. "Whoa, there, gorgeous. Where you goin' in such a hurry?"

"Let go of me!" I pushed past him.

The woman beside him, dressed in a low-cut red dress

and reeking of cheap perfume, crossed her arms. "Hey, Little Miss Stuck-up! He was just saving you from falling on your ass."

I didn't turn back. I just ran for my car.

"Faith!" Ethan's voice again. He'd followed me outside.

The woman sighed heavily. "What is wrong with people these days?" she said in frustration.

I fumbled with my keys, trying to get inside my car, but I knew it was too late. When his hands touched my shoulders, I whipped around and backed away. "Don't touch me."

He pulled his hands back and stretched them out to his sides. "I'm sorry. I didn't mean… What are you doing here?"

I studied the questioning look on his face. He was wearing jeans and a black T-shirt with the Spotted Cat logo in the upper left. His white apron was still tied around his waist, clean and ready for a night of work. And he looked good. Not like a man who had just been released from prison. Which was a stupid thought. What had I expected? A beard? A teardrop tattoo? Scars from fights with other prisoners?

Wind blew a strand of hair across my face, and I shoved it out of the way while turning my head into the cold breeze. My eyes watered, then emptied out. The wetness on my cheeks burned as it dried.

I turned back to him. "I didn't know you would be here." Or had I known? When I found that matchbook, had I subconsciously expected, or even hoped, to find Ethan here? Did some part of me *want* to see him? Had the happy memories overshadowed the ones that had destroyed our relationship forever?

My hands shook. I shivered more than the cool temperature warranted.

"You're terrified," he said. "After all this time, you're scared of me?"

I had no idea what to say. I didn't want to give this man the satisfaction of thinking I was scared of him. So I squared my shoulders. "I stopped being afraid of you twelve years ago."

"You're lying." He took a step forward. "But I won't hurt you. I was never the man the prosecutors and the media painted me to be. Surely you of all people know that. And I changed in prison."

At that, I laughed—a loud, hysterical laugh. "You changed?" I took a step closer to him, attempting to show him that I didn't fear him—a lie. "Well, me too. Stay away from me, Ethan. I promise to do the same."

I managed to unlock my car and slip inside even though my hands still shook. Ethan stood silently as I pulled out and turned back toward Paynes Creek.

But when I was a mile down the road, I pulled over into an empty church parking lot and let the tears I'd been holding flow. My entire body shook—an uncontrollable reaction to seeing Ethan up close and way-too-personal for the first time since he was sentenced eleven years ago. I let out a loud frustrated cry and beat a fist against the steering wheel. I had suspected I would see him sooner or later... but I had hoped it would be later.

I remembered how he looked in court every single day of his trial. What he wore, the glances he sent in my direction, those pleading eyes hoping to make contact with mine, the emotion on his face any time testimony didn't go his way. I remembered how he was continuously beaten down by the prosecutors, even though they never got the satisfaction of cross-examining him directly, as he chose not to testify on his own behalf. He never admitted guilt, but he also never revealed what he'd been doing just before his father and my mother were killed. He never told anyone how it was nearly impossible for him to have carried out the murders the way the prosecutors claimed.

Nearly impossible, but not absolutely so. A critical distinction.

My phone rang from inside my back pocket. After running the back of my hand across my tear-soaked face, I pulled my phone out and stared at the unfamiliar number. I took a couple of deep breaths and answered. "Faith Day."

"Faith, it's Luke. Would you mind meeting me at the station?"

"Why?" I concentrated on breathing and keeping my voice even.

"Well, since it's not a place I would typically take a woman on a date, I hoped it would be obvious that I'd like to ask you some questions."

"About?"

"You know, Miss Day, you should really work on your people skills. I'd like to go over some of the photos you took at the Reynolds fire. And I need to talk to you about Ethan Gentry."

I stretched my thumb and middle finger across my forehead and massaged my temples.

"You still there?" he asked. When I didn't answer, he said, "I'm sorry. It can't be easy to see your stepbrother released from prison. But I'm really trying to decide if he could possibly have anything to do with what's happening now."

He had no idea how hard it was for me to see Ethan released, and hopefully he never would. "I'll head that way."

"You okay? You sound… off."

"I'm fine. I'll be there in twenty."

I hung up and tossed the phone in the passenger seat. Who the hell was this Luke Justice? And how would I possibly get through this arson investigation if he continued to dig into the past?

———

THE STATION HOUSE was quiet that night. Small town. Small number of officers out on patrol. Even fewer officers at the station. I found Luke in one of the interrogation rooms. He had set up an evidence board on which were tacked photos, newspaper articles, and Post-It notes. He was concentrating so hard on something when I entered that he didn't even hear me. When I got closer, I realized he was staring at an article about Ethan's trial.

"You got me here, Special Agent. What can I help you with?" I scraped a metal chair against the concrete floor and sat, stuffing my hands into my coat pockets and crossing my outstretched legs at my ankles.

He jumped when I spoke, but recovered quickly. "Hi," he said warmly. "Did I tear you away from anything important?"

"Yes. What do you want?"

He eyed me curiously. "Is there a reason you're pretending you don't like me? Or is that how you treat everyone?"

I smiled then, but I felt fairly sure he found no warmth in it. "Is it important to you that I like you, Agent?"

He tilted his head side to side. "I'm not sure 'important' is the right word, but it would be helpful since we'll be working together. And I rather enjoyed the kiss you gave me yesterday."

Working together? On what planet does he think we'll be part-ners? How many times must I tell Chief Reid that I only take the

52

photos? I don't investigate, and I certainly don't work with hot-headed FBI agents.

"Besides, I'm a likable guy," he continued.

You're a smooth talker, that's for sure.

One of the night shift officers passed by the open door of the interview room and chuckled, apparently having overheard Luke flirting with me. Luke closed the door, then took a seat across the table from me. He opened a manila folder, pulled out a photograph, and slid it across the table for me to examine. "Tell me what you see in this photo."

I'd watched his reaction to the immature officer passing by, and the way he seemed to shift from playful to serious. It was interesting. *He* was interesting. But I certainly didn't want him to know I thought so.

"Is this a test?" I asked.

"Not at all. This is just me asking for your help. The Paynes Creek PD and the FBI would like your assistance, and we're willing to pay you for your time. I'm told you see things that others don't."

After analyzing his expression, I looked down at the photograph. It was definitely from an arson case, but not one I'd seen before. "Is this from another case you're investigating?"

He gave a simple nod.

I stared at the picture again. "I'm not an arson expert. It just looks like another house fire to me." I shrugged and slid the picture back to him.

"Now take a look at these." He moved a stack of several more photos toward me, all paper-clipped together.

I removed the paper clip and examined each picture. A few footprints. A close-up of fire damage to a wall left standing. A burned-out sofa.

When I flipped to the next one, my heart stopped. It was the remains of an animal. "A dog?"

Luke's jaw was rigid. He frowned. "Summer, the family's golden retriever."

I drilled the heel of my palm into my chest. It was difficult enough to work on murder investigations, but when defenseless children and pets were involved, it hurt my heart to its core.

Something about the photo caught my eye. "You have a loupe?"

He pulled a small black leather pouch from his bag, extracted a retractable magnifying glass from it, and handed it to me. "You see something?"

"Not sure." I held the loupe over a piece of metal lying next to the remains of the dog. It was a silver rabies tag in the shape of a dog bone, and thanks to the magnifying glass, I could just make out the name and phone number of Finch's veterinary clinic.

"What is it?" Luke asked, getting impatient.

I handed the magnifier back to him. "I thought it might be something, but…" I paused. "It was nothing." I leaned back and tucked my hands in my lap. "Where was this fire?"

He eyed me. Did he know I was hiding something? It wasn't that I wouldn't tell him, but I wanted to ask Finch about it first. Call it brother-sister loyalty or whatever.

"Two towns over. Midland."

"Midland." Why would Finch have a customer from Midland? "What were their names?"

"Missy and Dave Siegelman. Their daughter's name is Callie."

"Callie Siegelman," I said. "Why does that sound familiar?"

"Her family made a big deal of her daughter being

harassed by her high school administration for not turning over her phone when asked."

"She was propositioned by the art teacher. He wanted her to pose nude so he could paint her."

"That's the one," Luke said with the casual point of a finger. "That's what was alleged, anyway."

"How did that case end up?"

"The parents sued. There's a lot of gossip about it on online sites. But when the parents were killed in this fire, the story died with them. The teacher was stripped of his job, and he left town, not to be heard of again."

I sat back and crossed my arms. "And your other arson cases? Do they involve teens who were messing around with teachers?"

"No. But some involved women and girls in other… circumstances."

"Meaning?"

"They don't all involve teachers, but they involve some sort of sexual assault or inappropriate behavior between a man and a woman."

"Can you give me another example?" Why was he being so vague?

"Well, I discovered in one case that a woman had accused a coworker of sexually assaulting her at work. An executive of that company, Mark Shepherd, dismissed the accusations. Other coworkers interviewed said that Shepherd went as far as to promote the man accused, whereas the woman was moved into a lesser position. Shepherd is said to have told upper management that the woman had an overactive imagination and that her work wasn't what it used to be."

"He was looking to fire her," I said. "In order to get rid of the problem, he was going to punish the accuser instead of the predator."

"Exactly. And shortly after that, he was murdered—shot—and his car was set on fire."

"So—another case where the victim was killed by other means first, and then burned to cover up the evidence of the murder."

"One of the most common motives for arson."

"Crime concealment," I said, nodding. "But other than that, I don't see any connection to these other cases. Similar, but…" I left my statement hanging while I paused to consider what I might be missing. "Have you found any links between the victims?"

"We've been working on several theories, but no."

I studied the evidence board again. My hands grew clammy as I looked at the old articles about Ethan.

"Thought you weren't an investigator," Luke said with a smile.

"I'm not." I stood suddenly, realizing I had definitely shown too much interest. "Do you need anything else from me?"

Luke considered me a moment, then gathered up the photos, stood, and shoved them back into their folder. "I think that's enough for tonight." His mouth opened to say something else, but he stopped himself.

I nodded at the evidence board. "You seem awfully interested in Ethan's case. You think he had something to do with what's happening now?"

Luke turned and stared at the board for a long moment, then faced me again. "I'm investigating several fires that occurred after he was released from prison. But I have no hard evidence to place him at any of the scenes."

"Does he have alibis?"

"No, he lives alone and doesn't seem to have any social life. But we have people watching him now, so if another fire occurs…"

I tensed at his statement, and he had to see it, but I said nothing. Of course the FBI was watching Ethan. Which meant someone had to have told Luke that they saw me at the Spotted Cat.

Or they would soon.

SEVEN

It was after ten p.m. when I left the station. I hadn't eaten since lunch, and my mind was racing. Without thinking, I turned toward the neighborhood where my brother lived.

His vehicle was in the driveway. The porch light was out, but the glow of a television flashed in the living room window. I sat there for several minutes before deciding to confront him.

When I opened the car door, my phone buzzed. It was Luke again. Deciding I'd had enough of Luke Justice for one day, I sent the call to voicemail.

I knocked lightly on Finch's door. I heard movement and a crash—followed by cursing—before Finch opened the door. His chocolate lab, Sally Brown, danced behind him.

"Faith," he said, surprised. "What are you doing here?" He looked at his watch. "It's late."

"I saw Ethan."

He looked like he was trying to stifle a reaction at first, but then stepped aside. "Come in, but we have to keep it down. Aubrey hasn't been sleeping well. The second trimester was supposed to be easier, I thought."

I walked past him, through the foyer, and into the living room. Their house was decorated in soft beige and lots of white. Aubrey liked contemporary lines and modern art. And Finch liked whatever Aubrey liked.

"Is she doing okay? The baby's alright?" Finch and Aubrey had had trouble getting pregnant, so I couldn't help but worry for them.

"Yeah, she's fine. She's just been spending a lot of time volunteering at church lately. Too much time, if you ask me."

"Doing what?" I asked, curious.

"She's been counseling some people recently. Not sure who. She says she has to keep all that confidential."

"Oh, sure," I said.

Before getting pregnant, Aubrey had worked as a psychologist at an office in Lexington—she'd been there ever since interning as a college student. She'd even helped me find the therapist who diagnosed my hyperthymesia and helped me work through my issues after Mom was killed. But when she found out she was expecting, she and Finch decided they didn't really need her income, and she quit her job to concentrate on delivering a healthy baby.

"It's good that she's continuing to use her skills," I said.

"You going to tell me where you saw Ethan?" Finch asked.

Stalling, I rubbed Sally Brown's head. She was an older lab; Finch had owned her since he got his first apartment, sophomore year in college. She was still just a puppy when our mother died. "The Spotted Cat."

"In Lexington? What were you doing in a place like that?"

59

"It's a long story, but the fact is: I saw him. And I ran like a scared little girl."

Finch walked to me and enveloped me in his arms. He stood half a foot taller than me and was built like a rock. I leaned my forehead into his chest. His hugs were always exactly what I needed. "Of course you did. He hurt you more than any man should. And he shouldn't have been let out to hurt you again."

"Is it possible that he didn't kill them?"

"There was plenty of evidence to put him in prison."

"All circumstantial. And now he's out." But Uncle Henry and Chief Reid had always been so sure of Ethan's guilt.

"Ethan got exactly what he deserved," Finch said with finality.

"And yet, whatever this newly discovered evidence was... this exculpatory evidence... it was enough to convince the commonwealth's attorney to drop all charges."

"What did Ethan say to you?"

I shook my head while pressing my fingers into my tired eyes. "Nothing. I didn't really give him the opportunity." A chill moved along my arms, and I rubbed them.

"Come here, kiddo." Finch pulled me in for another squeeze. "I'm sorry he's out, but you need to stay away from him. If he's smart, he'll stay far away from us and this town."

I nodded into his chest. I hadn't known who I would find at the Spotted Cat. At least that's what I was telling myself. And I sure hadn't been prepared for him to run after me and try to talk to me.

I pulled back from Finch. "I'm gonna go. Sorry I came so late."

"You never have to apologize for that. You want to sleep in the guest room?"

"No. I need to get home to Gus."

"You know you're welcome here anytime."

I nodded. "I know. I'll call you tomorrow."

Finch grabbed a leash off the hook hanging just inside the kitchen. "I'll follow you out with Miss Sally, here."

I stepped out onto the porch. "I almost forgot. The FBI agent you met at the Reynoldses' wake… He showed me some photos tonight of another arson scene. A dog was killed, and wore tags that came from your clinic."

Finch's gaze narrowed, then he shrugged. "I'm sure vaccination tags from my clinic are spread all over the county."

"This one was over in Midland. You have any clients who bring their animals from Midland?"

"I'm sure I do." He smiled. "I'm a damn good vet. People come from all over to have their beloved pets cared for by the most charming veterinarian within a hundred miles." He gave my shoulder a light punch. "I'm sure Mr. Justice will be by to talk, and I'll help him in any way I can. But like I said, evidence of my veterinary prowess can be found all over Kentucky."

I scoffed. "Humble much, big brother? But yeah, you're right. I'm being silly."

EIGHT

I lay in bed that night remembering every detail of the day I first met Ethan. He had just moved to Paynes Creek with his father.

I entered Miss Miller's English class on the third day of eighth grade. My best friend Amy and I had been insepa-rable all summer. We stumbled into the room, laughing, and found our seats next to each other just as the bell rang. Miss Miller was writing something across the dry erase board when I noticed the new boy. He was sitting on the opposite side of me from Amy. He was thin, with long legs, and his navy, Chuck Taylor–covered feet stretched out in front of him. He looked relaxed, not nervous like most newcomers would feel. His hair was short in the back, but his bangs hung messily across his forehead.

I nudged Amy with my foot, then lifted my head in the boy's direction. She lifted her brows in recognition of the cute boy. We weren't that into boys yet—at least, not in an obvious way—but we liked to talk about them when they weren't around. And this one was an interesting addition to the school. We hadn't had anyone new in our tiny town in a long time.

When the bell rang after class, I grabbed my books and stood. I was about to follow Amy out the door when Tabitha Blake, a bitchy cheerleader, walked over. She shoved me backward and out of her way, knocking my books out of my hands. "Oh, sorry. I didn't see you there, Faith." She continued on over to the new boy. "Want to walk me to my next class?"

The new boy just stared at her. No smile. His dark brows stayed straight. There was no humor in his eyes.

"Are you mute?" Tabitha said. I could only watch as she went from acting like a confident flirt to a dramatic bitch.

He studied her for one second more, then let his eyes drift slowly in my direction. He took a step over to me. Bending down, he picked up my books and handed them to me. "You okay?" he asked.

I nodded, unable to speak.

Tabitha blew out a frustrated growl, then spun around and stormed out of the room.

Amy, who had been waiting for me, burst out laughing. She ran up to the new boy. "That was amazing. I'm Amy. This is Faith. You just moved here."

"Yeah. My dad and me. I'm Ethan."

"Well, it's nice to meet you, Ethan." Amy bumped me.

"Oh, yeah," I said. "Good to meet you, Ethan. And thanks for that."

"No problem." He grabbed his books and headed for the door. Just as he was about to leave, he turned back. "I'll see you around, Faith."

NINE

I spent the entire next day hiding from reality—cleaning my home and working on a couple of side projects. My phone rang a few times during the afternoon, but after verifying it wasn't Chief Reid or someone from the station, I ignored the calls, paranoid that Ethan was attempting to reach me.

At around six in the evening, I lit two candles and poured myself a drink, and I was about to settle in with a sexy paranormal romance novel about witches and vampires when an unwelcome knock sounded at my door.

Sighing, I rose and opened it.

Luke stood just outside. Concern was etched in the trenches of his forehead, and there was a stiffness in his jaw—though it relaxed when he saw me.

"Something wrong, Agent?"

"Don't you answer your phone?"

"As a matter of fact I do... *when* I recognize the caller and feel like talking to people." I shrugged. "I didn't feel very social today." I stood in the doorway, looking down at him. He was a good-looking guy, muscular in all the right places, with a thick head of dark hair. This was not a man who was going to go bald any time soon. I almost chuckled at the thought. Why did I care if he went bald? Besides, he'd still look good with no hair.

Down, Faith. The bourbon must have been kicking in.

"You have another one of those?" He nodded toward my drink.

"Another one of what? The cup or what's in it?"

"Both."

I stepped back, giving him room to step up into my tiny home. When Gus rubbed against his shins and wove in between his legs, he stooped down and said hello, giving her a scratch behind her ears. One point for Luke. Anyone who liked Gus and wasn't greeted by an angry hiss passed the first test, a feat not often accomplished.

"Who's this?" he asked, standing.

Gus sat and began licking her hind leg.

"Gus. I rescued her."

"Gus is a 'her'?"

"I named her before I took her in to Finch to be fixed. He informed me that I had the sex wrong." I shrugged. "The name had already stuck. It's short for Asparagus." When he gave me a strange look, I explained. "You know, from *Cats*, the musical?" I gave my head a shake when he still looked confused. "Never mind."

He looked around my trailer, then faced me with a curious grin. "This is not at all what I expected when I heard you lived in a trailer out in the country."

"An Airstream," I corrected.

"A what?" he asked, then seemed to understand. "Oh, yeah. A specific type of trailer. But this..." He looked around again. "This is amazing. Cozy. Decorated. Not at all what my grandparents took me camping in when I was a kid. And certainly not the tornado magnet double-wide us city slickers envision when thinking of Kentucky."

"Thank you. I built it myself."

"You what?" An eyebrow shot up as he considered me.

"This is a 1969 Airstream that I gutted and remodeled. Everything in this 'trailer'—as you like to call it—was carefully selected or custom-built and installed by me," I tilted my head side to side, "with a little help from two very special people in my life." Namely my uncle and Finch, but I wanted to be vague to throw Luke off-balance, make him wonder if I had a romantic someone or two in my life.

"It's very impressive."

I pulled down a sterling silver julep cup from a cabinet, added an oversized ice cube from a mold in the freezer, and opened the bottle of bourbon I had chosen for the evening.

"That's an awfully fancy cup."

I shrugged. "It's a bourbon worthy of fancy."

"How did a woman living in a trailer come to own expensive barware? Did you inherit them?"

I couldn't stop the grin that lifted the corners of my lips. "I turned tricks to pay my way through college. When I made a little extra, I put it toward barware worthy of a one-hundred-fifty-dollar bottle of bourbon."

He cocked his head. "You were *not* a prostitute."

I gave him a sardonic smile in answer, then drizzled a couple of ounces of bourbon over the ice.

"Also, that bourbon cost one fifty?" His voice rose an octave. Either he'd surmised I was joking about turning tricks, or he didn't care.

I nodded. "Does that make you want the drink even more now?"

"It kind of does." His eyes lit up like a kid on his birthday.

When I handed Luke the drink, his fingers grazed over mine and seemed to linger a bit longer than necessary. I lifted my eyes to meet his, then drew my hand back. "What brings you all the way out to my home, Agent Justice?"

He set the bourbon aside, almost as if thinking better of accepting the drink. His face was more serious. "Why didn't you tell me that you went to see your brother?"

My spine straightened, and I tried to bury any outward reaction on my face. "Finch? I haven't even seen you since then. And I had no idea the FBI would be interested in when and if I saw my brother."

"You know I'm talking about Ethan."

"Uh… no, I didn't." Except that I did. "Ethan is not my brother. He *was* my stepbrother… until he killed his father and my mother. Then he simply became the man who murdered my mom."

"Fine." Frustration coated the word. "Why didn't you mention that you'd seen Ethan Gentry when we spoke last night?"

"Because it simply didn't come up. And because I was still trying to recover from the shock of seeing Ethan."

"So you were shocked? You didn't know that he was working at the Spotted Cat?"

I took a drink of bourbon and considered Luke for a long moment. "I'm only going to ask you one more time: why are you here, Special Agent Justice?" I spat the words "Special Agent" to remind him that he was here, inside my home, in an official capacity. And that he probably shouldn't be enjoying my bourbon if he planned to interrogate me.

"You know I'm looking into Ethan's case, and that we're watching him. And when I found out that one of my agents had seen Ethan arguing with a woman that fit your description outside the Spotted Cat, I got… concerned."

"You got concerned," I deadpanned.

"Yes. And curious."

"Ahh," I said, unable to hide my patronizing tone. "You were curious about how I knew that my former step-brother was working at the Spotted Cat."

"Yes. So tell me, and we can get back to enjoying our drink."

I tipped back my glass of bourbon, maybe to prove that I didn't need his permission to have a drink. "Well, like I already said, I was surprised to see Ethan at the Spotted Cat." Since it seemed we were going to have a conversation whether I liked it or not, I grabbed Luke's bourbon, squeezed past him, lingering as I passed—my chest facing his—and took a seat in one of the booths at my kitchen table. I gestured for Luke to have a seat across from me. He did. "I get the impression you're a good inves-tigator, that you ask a lot of questions whether they seem relevant at the time or not. And since you alluded to hearing things about me, I assume you asked around at the precinct, and are well aware that I called the station last week to report that someone had broken into my trailer and set a fire on my property."

He looked in the direction of my fire pit, which told me not only did he know about the fire, he knew exactly where my fire pit was located. And as it was dark out right now, there was no way he'd just happened to see the pit on his way in. "I read the report, and yes, I talked to some people."

"And you heard the officers around the station debate my sanity. Maybe I built the fire myself, and then forgot that I'd moved some things around my home. Maybe I called it in to get attention."

"Yes, I've heard the talk." Luke had the decency to look embarrassed that he'd listened to petty, station-house gossip. "But I didn't believe it. What does that have to do with the Spotted Cat?"

"Another fire was set a few mornings ago."

"Here?" Concern was back in his expression.

"Yes. And they broke into my trailer again."

"What? Did you call it in?"

"Call it in? To the same police officers who are laughing behind my back? You think those guys would have rushed out here to protect and serve me?"

"Why do you care what they think?"

"It's not that I care. I just don't like being talked about. I've been gossiped about for most of my life." I closed my eyes for a beat, then gave my head a little shake in an attempt to push back the memories. It was no use, of course. "Anyway, after the latest fire was set, I discovered a matchbook from the Spotted Cat. It was just lying there beside one of the log benches."

"So you thought you would just go to the lounge, and what? Listen to some jazz music and hope someone you recognized strolled in and admitted that they got off on building bonfires on your property and rummaging through your things?" Luke's voice took on an edge.

I angled my head while letting a grin play at the corners of my lips. Luke sounded protective. "Are you angry with me, Agent? That's cute."

His eyes narrowed at the word "cute." "Why aren't you taking this seriously?"

"I'm taking it very seriously. I reported it the first time. The police told me since they found no evidence of an actual crime, they could do nothing for me. Said it was probably just a couple of high school kids playing a prank. That I probably had left my door unlocked."

"What days did these fires occur?" He pulled a small black notebook and pen from his pocket.

"This past Wednesday and a week ago Sunday. Both were set in the early morning hours. Around four a.m. each time."

"That's awfully exact," he said.

"I have an awfully exact memory of things that happen to me."

He seemed to let that go. He was jotting a quick note as I spoke, then looked up and met my gaze. "Those are mornings after two of the house fires were set—the Midland fire and the Reynolds fire last week."

I lifted my drink to him. "Yes. Coincidence?"

"I'm an FBI agent. I don't believe in coincidences until they're proven to be."

"One of those fires was two counties over."

"True. They also occurred after Ethan was released from prison." He reached out a hand and traced the condensation running down the julep cup. "Care to tell me more about him?"

"Is this still a professional call, Special Agent Justice?"

Luke lifted the bourbon I'd fixed him and took a sip. After swallowing, he closed his eyes, clearly savoring the taste in his mouth. When he opened his eyes, he locked on to my gaze. "The moment I accepted this drink, I went off the clock."

"Good. I don't want to talk about Ethan. I'll be happy to tell you about him in the light of day when I'm sober." *When I can be more careful with my words.*

He took another drink, then examined the cup. "So *that's* what one-hundred-fifty-dollar bourbon tastes like out of sterling silver."

"I found that cup at an estate auction. Won the bid on three julep cups that day. I was bidding against some old man who owns an antique store in town. He was pissed when I won, but congratulated me after and invited me to coffee to explain to me exactly what I had purchased." I shrugged. "He and I became great friends that day."

"Didn't you already know what you were purchasing?"

"At three hundred dollars apiece? Of course I knew what I was purchasing. But it gave him a great big belly laugh when I explained that I just wanted some cups for my moonshine that wouldn't break when I moved my trailer around."

Luke laughed at that—a warm, kind laugh. The kind a woman would love to hear every single day of her life.

"So tell me," I said. "Where does Luke Justice live when he's not chasing criminals?"

"I technically live in a townhouse outside Quantico, Virginia. My unit is based out of the academy there."

"You're with the Behavioral Analysis Unit." I had thought about applying to the academy once upon a time, but thought better of it.

"I am. Technically, I'm part of the National Center for the Analysis of Violent Crimes. I usually investigate arson, but I'm also a forensic psychologist and help with serial killer investigations."

I stood as he spoke, walked to the kitchen, grabbed the bottle of bourbon, and brought it back to the table. As he went on about how he traveled the country to consult with state and local police and fire departments on investigations, I poured us both more bourbon.

"Sounds like you enjoy your job, Agent."

He reached across the table and placed a hand over mine. I looked up, surprised.

"I liked it better when you called me Luke," he said. "It's nice not to be at a bar or restaurant, and in someone's home instead."

I pulled my hand back and tapped my cup to his.

"Here's to you not being the workaholic I thought you were."

He, too, pulled his hand back, but not before flashing a look of disappointment. "This doesn't mean I won't be back tomorrow to question you further about Ethan, but for tonight…"

"For tonight you're going to enjoy my expensive bourbon."

"Oh, I think I'm enjoying much more than that."

"Don't get any ideas, Agent. I'm not going to sleep with you." I kept my eyes on his as I shifted slightly in my seat.

"Your eyes and your body language tell a different tale."

I looked at him again. "Okay, Mr. Profiler. What do my eyes and body say?"

"That you don't think you *should* sleep with me, but that you're pretty sure you will. Eventually."

"Want to know what *your* body language suggests to *me?*"

"What?"

"That your arrogance gets you into trouble."

He tilted his head side to side. "Or maybe it says my confidence will get me what I want."

"A fleeting desire. One that will deliver regret."

"Are you scared to find out?"

"I don't frighten that easily." A lie.

He threw back the rest of his bourbon, then stood and took a step toward me. Reaching down, he grabbed my hand and pulled me to my feet. He slid a hand to the back of my neck. "I've wanted to do this ever since you made the first move at Boone's." He leaned his head to one side, then the other.

He was about to lean in and kiss me when I said, "That was a mistake. I shouldn't have kissed you."

"Mistake or not, I was sorry you didn't stick around that night." He covered my mouth with his, a gentle kiss that tasted of warm caramel and a hint of oak with a slight burn of alcohol. As he deepened the kiss, I felt the movement of his tongue against my lower lip, and I knew I was in trouble.

My hand went to his side, and I squeezed a handful of his shirt in my fist.

He broke the kiss first. "I'm a patient man," he whispered with a voice that was fluid like smoke. He stood close, his face inches from mine. I could feel the heat of his breath against my face. I didn't dare breathe. "Thanks for the bourbon."

And then he turned and left, leaving me questioning everything I'd ever learned about men.

TEN

I spent the first part of the next morning replaying Luke's kiss. While I spent a lot of time reliving bad memories, it was nice to have something good to throw in the mix every once in a while. And the kiss had definitely been... mind-blowingly good.

I'd skipped breakfast, and by eleven o'clock I was starving, craving caffeine, and needing some painkillers for the headache I was nursing. But I'd gotten hung up at the courthouse. It was day two of a trial to convict three men charged with selling drugs—crack cocaine, prescription narcotics, synthetic narcotics, and prefabricated fentanyl pills—within a thousand feet of a school. As a witness for the prosecution, I sat behind their bench, so I was able to overhear the attorneys remark that two of the accused had turned on the third, and the prosecutors were in the process of offering a plea deal to the two who were now cooperating. Unfortunately, until an agreement was reached, the trial would continue.

I was called to the stand around eleven thirty. I testified to the validity of the photographs I'd taken of one of the accused's cars, including pictures of the drugs and para-phernalia. My testimony was typically only a formality to validate what could be seen in the photographs. But in this case, the defense for one of the accused—the owner of the vehicle—was claiming that his client had been set up.

"Miss Day, how soon after the arrest of my client were you called to the scene?"

I leaned into the microphone. "According to the police report, I was called within thirty minutes of the arrest."

The attorney, who was not from Paynes Creek, held up a report and introduced it into evidence. Then he walked closer to me, smiled in a very condescending manner, and clasped his hands in front of him. "Miss Day," he said, angling his head. "Would there have been time in those thirty minutes for someone to have planted the drugs and 'evidence' in my client's vehicle?" He placed air quotes around the word "evidence."

I looked at the arresting officer, William Puckett, who was seated in the third row of the courtroom awaiting his turn to take the stand. He rubbed a hand over his bald head; the line of darker stubble in a crescent shape just beneath the skin suggested baldness was a choice he'd made when his hairline began to recede. He was an arro-gant but well-respected officer who was hoping to make detective soon, and most likely would.

I redirected my gaze back to the defense attorney. "No, sir."

"No?" The attorney acted surprised at my answer. "How can you be so sure?"

"There wasn't enough time, and it was broad daylight at a busy gas station."

"That sounds like your opinion, Miss Day."

I glanced uneasily at the prosecutor, then the judge, then back at the defense attorney. "Correct me if I'm wrong, but I thought that was the reason I was on the stand. As an expert with an opinion."

A sprinkle of chuckles erupted in the courtroom followed by an "Order!" from the judge. "Miss Day, you'll answer the question based on the facts."

"Yes, ma'am. I apologize." It wasn't a very sincere apology, seeing as I didn't see what I had done wrong. I met the attorney's gaze again. "I'm sorry, what was the question?"

A few more chuckles could be heard. Officer Puckett ran his hand across his mouth, unable to fully hide a snicker.

"Can you give us the exact timeline as it is detailed in the police report leading up to your arrival on the scene?"

"The arresting officer pulled the three accused over at three fifteen in the afternoon, just after school had been let out. There was a steady flow of high school students driving and walking in and out of the gas station. I was on the scene by three forty-five, at which time witnesses were being interviewed. It is my expert opinion, based on the facts, that the vehicle holding evidence of the crimes had not been touched between the time of the arrest and when I arrived."

The questioning went on and on with the defense attorney trying to get me to suggest that I had photographed planted evidence.

When I was finally excused from the stand, Officer Puckett watched me make my way from the courtroom. He seemed to want to make eye contact with me and communicate in some way, but I barely gave him a glance. He was one of the officers who'd taken my statement after the first fire on my property.

In the hallway outside the courtroom, people gathered in corners, waiting on one thing or another. Attorneys paced with their cell phones to their ears. I could always pick out the attorneys by the suits they wore.

Someone grabbed my hair and pulled me backward. "You stupid bitch!" a woman screamed.

I stumbled backwards, my hand going to the back of my head, trying to lessen the pain. The woman was pulling *hard*.

"That dirty cop has had it in for my Mickey for years."

I managed to look up at the woman. Frizzy hair in curlers framed her face, and thick wrinkles accentuated black eyes, darkened by furrowed, angry brows.

"Your Mickey is an addict who sells drugs to children," I said.

She pulled harder, then punched me in the cheekbone.

Puckett appeared behind the woman and wrapped his arms around her, forcing her to let go of my hair. In seconds he had her on the ground, a knee in her back and cuffs on her wrists.

"You okay?" he asked me.

I nodded, rubbing my jaw and feeling for any loose teeth.

Reinforcements arrived, and he stood, reached out a hand, and helped me up. He shot me a look of respect—and maybe even gratitude—for backing him up in the courtroom. What he probably didn't understand was that I had no idea if he was a dirty cop or not. I simply answered as honestly as I could.

My phone buzzed in my back pocket. I took one look at it, then wiggled it at Officer Puckett. "The station. Gotta go."

"Put some ice on that cheek. It's already starting to swell."

As I WALKED into the station, Matthew Lake was sitting outside one of the interview rooms. Luke exited the chief's office and was headed in Matthew's direction when he saw me. His eyes narrowed. He motioned for an officer and gave him an order I couldn't hear. The officer turned and led Matthew into the interview room. Luke then walked over to me.

His fingers went immediately to my cheekbone. They were cool against my bruised skin. "What happened?"

I pulled back, quickly looking around to see who was watching. Luke followed my gaze, then took a step back as realization set in.

"Who did that to you?" Anger was in his voice this time.

"A white trash woman in curlers, if you can believe it." I did my best to let my lips curve into a smile as I grabbed my head. "She managed to pull hard on a chunk of my hair, too."

His lips tightened into a thin line before he spoke again. "Your face needs ice. Go get some, then go to the observation room. I'm about to question Matthew Lake."

"For what?"

"For killing the Reynoldses and setting fire to the house to cover it up."

"You think he did that?"

"He certainly has motive. Without the parents, there's no one to pursue charges against him for statutory rape and inappropriate contact with a minor. The prosecutor won't pursue it without a lot more evidence."

"I'm not buying it."

"What are you doing tonight?" he asked. An abrupt change of subject.

I cocked my head. "Why?"

He smiled. "I'd like to ask you out to dinner."

"No," I said quickly. Maybe a little too quickly. "That's a really bad idea." I glanced around the station again.

"Okay then. You think about it. I'm going to go question the idiot"—he thumbed over his shoulder—"and I'll talk to you after."

I watched him go. He turned and gave me a look before he entered the interview room. I admired the way he looked in dress slacks, a button-down shirt with sleeves rolled to his elbows, and another silk tie, this one with tiny baby blue elephants. I suspected he had a sports jacket around here somewhere and could transform into looking one hundred percent professional if necessary, but this relaxed look told suspects that he was flustered and ready to throw the book at someone. It was intimidating.

I felt someone slide up behind me. "So... what's going on with you and Mr. Hot FBI Agent?"

It was Penelope, of course, and I could hear the hopeful excitement in her voice.

I was about to deny anything happening, but as I soon as I turned to face her, Penelope flinched at the sight of me. "Oh, honey!"

"I know." I grabbed her arm. "Help me find some ice."

I dragged her to the station kitchen and let her fill a sandwich bag with ice.

"What are you doing tonight?" I asked.

"I have no plans. Why?" She handed me the bag.

I already felt guilty for using her. "Want to have dinner with me?"

"Oh, I don't know," she said, long and drawn out. "The last time you and I went out drinking, I was hung over for two days. And hubsy-wubsy was not happy with either of us."

"Hubsy-wubsy?" A smirk played at the corners of my

lips. "Well, this time we'll just have dinner. My treat. We need a girls' night. It's been a while."

She looked like she still needed convincing.

I placed the ice bag against my face, wincing when it touched the fresh bruise. "Okay. The truth is, I need a reason to say no to Mr. Hot FBI Agent."

"Why would you say no to him?" She said this rather too loudly, then stretched her neck to see if anyone was outside the door. "Why don't you want to go out with him?"

"Why would I say yes? He's in town for one case, then he's gone. I'm not good for him. And I have no desire to feed the gossip train."

"Look, I've met him. And I've met all the other arrogant jerks of Paynes Creek. This guy is different. He might be just what you need."

I knew better. Luke Justice was looking for information to connect the death of my mom to the recent arsons and murders. Did I really want him using me to do that?

"Please go out with me," I pleaded. I gave Penelope a pouty face very uncharacteristic of me.

"Fine. Boone's. Six thirty. But for the record, *I* think you should go out with Mr. Hot FBI Agent."

FIFTEEN MINUTES LATER, armed with an ice pack, I walked into the observation room. Luke was already questioning Matthew on the other side of the one-way glass, and Chief Reid was standing on my side of the window, his arms crossed, watching the interview.

Chief lifted a brow when he saw me. "I heard you got clobbered at the courthouse today. You okay?"

"I'm fine." I didn't elaborate, and Chief didn't question further.

Luke was leaning across a table, his back to us, staring into Matthew's face. Matthew was sitting straight up in his chair, looking scared to death. His lawyer sat next to him, casually making notes on a legal pad.

"So you're telling me that you were with Bella Reynolds the night her parents were murdered," Luke said. "But you're denying that you and Bella are having any kind of physical relationship that would be construed as... inappropriate."

"You don't have to answer that," Matthew's attorney said with barely a glance up. "Agent, Mr. Lake has already spoken to the nature of his purely platonic relationship with Ms. Reynolds. I'm tiring of this line of questioning. And when I tire completely, we leave."

"Fair enough." Luke straightened. "Mr. Lake, tell me about the last time you were invited into the Reynoldses' home."

I leaned forward, wincing when I knocked the ice against my bruise a little too hard.

Matthew looked over at his attorney, who nodded his approval to answer the question.

"The Reynoldses have had me to their home on numerous occasions. The last time I went, I gave Bella a piano lesson, and then Mrs. Reynolds fixed dinner."

"Did you drink while you were there?"

Matthew again looked at his attorney before answering. "Only after Bella's lesson. The Reynoldses were very kind to me."

"Did Bella drink?" Luke asked.

"Yes, the Reynoldses believed that teaching their daughter to drink responsibly in a social situation was a good thing. If teens are going to drink anyway, they felt they should teach Bella the importance of moderation and drinking responsibly."

"Did you smoke marijuana while in the Reynoldses' home?"

Luke must have had reason to believe that Matthew smoked pot with the Reynoldses, or he wouldn't have asked the question.

The attorney's eyebrows shot up. "Special Agent Justice, you've asked that my client cooperate. Asking him to confess to another crime does not help him, and pissing me off with this line of questioning won't help *you*."

Luke changed tack. "You say the Reynoldses were kind to you," he said. "I'm assuming you mean they were kind *until* they accused you of inappropriate behavior with their daughter."

The attorney lifted his head again. He appeared to be about to object when Matthew blurted out, "They wouldn't have made those claims had others not pressured them. They were in the process of withdrawing their allegations when…" He trailed off.

"When they were killed?" Luke asked—rather harshly.

The attorney stood. "We are finished here. Don't—"

"I didn't kill them," Matthew said, his voice climbing.

"But you did accept bribes from them. And marijuana, which is illegal in the state of Kentucky."

"If you call dinner and drinks bribes…"

The attorney had lost control of his client. "Don't answer any more—"

"I do," Luke said quickly, cutting off the lawyer. "They wined and dined you and provided you with marijuana, and you promised what? Scholarships for Bella? An audition at Juilliard? Did you promise other girls these kinds of things? What else did these girls give you in exchange for these empty promises?"

When Matthew's attorney slammed his pen against his legal pad, Luke backed up a step with his hands in the air. "Fine. I withdraw those questions for now."

Matthew was breathing hard, and his face was red.

Could Matthew even deliver on such promises? I wondered. Not that it mattered. All that would matter was whether Bella or her parents believed that he could.

I analyzed Matthew's body language. He linked and unlinked his hands. He leaned forward in the seat, then back. He was frustrated.

"Who pressured the Reynoldses?" Luke asked. "You said someone pressured them. What did you mean by that? Who knew that you were 'helping' Bella?"

Matthew stood suddenly, knocking his metal chair backward onto the tiled floor. "Bella will *earn* scholarships and an audition with Juilliard on her *own merits*. I—"

"Say nothing further, Matthew!" The attorney practically yelled this time.

"Who else have you promised this special attention?" Luke asked. "Isn't it true that Alexandra Sims and Sadie Porter were both promised scholarships to your alma mater if they would send you pictures of themselves?"

"What?" Matthew said. "I did no such thing. Those two girls—"

"Matthew!" his attorney boomed. "Agent Justice, we are done here. If you have a reason to arrest my client, do it now. Otherwise, we are leaving."

Luke backed up and leaned against the wall. "You're free to go any time you'd like. You always were." But before Matthew could get the door open, Luke said, "Oh, just one more question: do you know the Siegelmans from Midland, Kentucky?"

Matthew turned. "Who?"

"Missy and Dave Siegelman? Or their daughter, Callie?"

I studied Matthew's face. There, etched in the lines that formed between his furrowed brows and in the hardness of his jaw, was the slightest hint of recognition.

"Never heard of them."

And he walked out.

ELEVEN

I left the station without speaking to Luke. He was tied up in Chief Reid's office, most likely discussing and analyzing the interview with Matthew.

The Paynes Creek Police Department was adjacent to the Hopewell County Public Library. Across the street was a city park, and the high school was just a few blocks away. Back in my teen years, Ethan and I would usually walk from school straight to the library or the park, depending on the weather, where we would hang out and do home-work until Mom could pick us up. Sometimes friends would join us, but often it was just the two of us.

The park was where we smoked marijuana for the first time. We were sophomores. A friend of Ethan's had given him a joint, and we decided that we would try it together.

"I'll go first," he had said. "If I get sick or something, you can take me to the hospital and tell everyone you tried to talk me out of it."

But he didn't get sick. We both smoked the joint, and we laughed harder than we'd ever laughed before. That was the day that Ethan admitted to me that he'd tried to talk his father out of marrying my mother.

"Why would you do that?" I asked. "They're in love. And they're so happy. And now we're brother and sister." We were sitting on the swings, which had just been installed that year. I loved how Ethan would grab hold of my swing, pull me to him, then let go. I would swing awkwardly sideways, then back until I slammed into him.

Ethan took the joint from me and seemed to consider the fact that we were now brother and sister. After inhaling deeply, he passed the joint back. "I don't want to be your brother. I thought you and I would end up together eventually."

When my head jerked toward his, his eyes burned into mine. He was no longer laughing.

My smile faltered, and I choked a little on the pot smoke I had just sucked in. "You're kidding, right?" I asked, coughing. "We were always just… friends."

"We *had* been friends, but I was going to ask you to the homecoming dance our freshman year. And not as a friend. But then my dad told me he was going to ask your mom to marry him, and he said that under no uncertain circumstances was I to make a move on you. He told me my feelings were just silly teenage feelings, and that they would go away."

"I remember that dance," I said. "I went with Pukey Phillip Pearse."

Ethan laughed. It was under his breath, and it didn't seem sincere. "I know. I told him to ask you."

I punched Ethan's upper arm, trying to bring the conversation back to light and airy. "Why did you do that? I didn't like him at all."

"I know you didn't." He smiled. "But I knew you

wouldn't hurt his feelings. And I knew I wouldn't be jealous of Pukey Phillip Pearse."

"You shouldn't have done that."

"My dad was wrong. My feelings aren't going away." Ethan held my swing in place, close to him. His hand rested along the inside of my thigh, his thumb rubbing a spot just above my knee. "Just for one moment, I want to remember the fact that we aren't related by blood and pretend that our parents' marriage hasn't made us family."

His eyes were the color of midnight, and they bored into mine with a look of lust. No, not lust. *Love.* Ethan loved me. And in that moment, high on a tiny amount of marijuana, I thought that Ethan and I would always have a bond. We would always be connected. But we would never act on the feelings we shared.

Ethan later blamed his confession on the marijuana; he said he clearly hadn't been of his right mind. But he never denied the truth of his words, and it wouldn't be the last time he would profess feelings for me.

When Mom picked us up that day, we giggled all the way home. She never said a word about the marijuana—not even when we ate every piece of junk food we could find, then insisted on making our own dinner right away.

But she knew.

TWELVE

Aunt Leah and Uncle Henry lived in a historic home —white clapboard with a matching white picket fence—built in 1893. It wasn't far from the heart of Paynes Creek. Uncle Henry liked living near the city fire station, and Aunt Leah was passionate about historic buildings.

I knocked first out of respect and as a warning, but then I opened the front door and yelled to Aunt Leah. She always got mad when I didn't just come on in. *This is your home*, she always said. *You never have to knock here.* But because I was now an adult, and no longer lived with them, I felt they didn't need me barging in unannounced.

And I hadn't really lived here long—though it had felt like it at the time. They had helped me through months of therapy as I dealt with losing my mom, stepfather, and Ethan. I'd actually been seeing a therapist since even before Mom died—a therapist Aubrey suggested, because Aubrey was interning at her office while finishing her undergraduate degree—but the therapy became a lot more intense that last year of high school. In college, I returned to Uncle Henry's and Aunt Leah's during the summers, but I moved out as soon as I could afford it. Well, afford it with Finch's help. He knew I needed my own space.

"Aunt Leah!" I yelled again as I entered the house.

"Back here," she called.

I found her in her office in the back of the house. She did the bookkeeping for several small businesses around Paynes Creek, including a beauty shop, Bryn's Coffeehouse, Finch's veterinary office, a local feed store, and other businesses typical of a rural farm community. Stopping into the beauty shop and Bryn's Coffeehouse twice a week kept her up on all the gossip.

I gave the top of her head a kiss.

"What brings you by today?" she asked.

"Do I need a reason to stop by and see my favorite aunt?"

"I'm your only aunt," she said, continuing to work. Her eyes darted from her calculator to a yellow legal pad, where she recorded an amount. Then she set her calculator aside and peered at me over a pair of zebra-print readers perched on the end of her nose. Her eyes widened. "What happened to you?"

My fingers brushed my bruised cheekbone. "Oh, it's nothing. I upset the mother of an accused drug trafficker in court today. Apparently she thought I was unfair in my assessment of her 'baby's' guilt." I didn't bother to hide my sarcasm.

"Did you ice it?"

"Yes. I'm fine." I waved her off. "Aunt Leah, you remember the night Mom was killed?" I closed my eyes a second. "What am I saying? Of course you remember. But do you remember the details? I didn't attend the entire trial, so I never actually got to hear Ethan's side of things —or at least what the attorney argued, since Ethan never took the stand. And the media's coverage was so biased."

"Biased? Ethan murdered your mother and his father in cold blood. He burned down the house to get rid of the evidence that would point to him."

"But he pulled me out of the fire. Did you ever wonder why he saved my life?"

"Why are you bringing this up now? Has he come back to town?"

I quickly shook my head. "No. Nothing like that." I didn't want to tell Aunt Leah I had seen Ethan. I didn't want to worry her. "It's just, I'm trying to figure out some things. Despite this new evidence that caused him to be released, I still think he probably set the fire, but... why would he bother to save me if there was even a chance that I witnessed him setting the fire?"

"Well, honey, I like to think there's good in everyone. Ethan simply had more bad than good. The bad came out when he was angry at his father and your mother for whatever reason—but the good side came out with you. He probably didn't mean for you to get caught up in the crossfire." She turned and resumed her work as if this were just a normal, everyday conversation.

"Maybe." I knew Ethan had his share of darkness affecting his soul. But with his recent release from prison, and now these fires, I found myself questioning a lot of the details from that night.

Aunt Leah turned again. "How about we have some iced tea? You can take a look at this year's proposal for the downtown Christmas decorations."

"Is that your way of changing the subject?"

"Yes. Did it work?"

I smiled. "I'd be happy to take a look at the decorations. I'd love to make sure the decorations are tasteful and elegant and not the tacky lights that Mrs. Silverson put up a few years ago."

"Oh, I know," Aunt Leah said. "Weren't those awful?"

We both laughed. I put my arm around her, and we headed for the kitchen. She hadn't taken the place of my mother, but she sure had softened the blow of losing two of the most important people in my life.

I WAS restless after my visit with Aunt Leah. She was always good at calming me, but she was also an expert at avoiding the subject of that night. And how could I blame her? She'd had to pick up the pieces left behind. Uncle Henry, too. He was devastated at having to investigate the fire that killed his only sister, but he still found it in him to console me. My mother had been my rock. She was everything to me.

I was on my way to Boone's Taphouse to meet Penelope—a little early, but I would wait at the bar—when she sent me a text.

Sorry! Have to cancel. Danny threw up all over me after daycare. Temp 103.

The text about her ill three-year-old son was followed by several sick-faced emojis.

So much for girls' night.

I took a turn and headed toward home. But when I got to the street that would take me to my house, I found myself turning left instead of right—toward the neighboring property. Although it was now inhabited by former FBI Agent Cooper Adams, everyone still called it the "Kuster Farm," after old Mr. Kuster. Rumor had it that Cooper had been working with a renovation crew when Mr. Kuster decided to sell, so Cooper purchased it, and had lived there ever since.

It was also where Luke was staying while he was in town.

I pulled into the drive. The porch light was on, and I could see the glow of a light toward the back of the house. "This is stupid," I said to myself. "What am I doing?" I had no excuse for being here; I didn't even know Cooper that well. He was my brother's age, but he and my brother had never been that close. And I had turned down Luke's offer of dinner. Three times.

Before I could talk myself out of it, I got out of my vehicle and stepped up onto the front porch—a traditional southern porch that stretched the entire width of the house and begged for a porch swing. It looked like renovation was still underway—though most of the porch was covered in chipped paint, some portions were now raw, unpainted wood. I couldn't help but think Cooper had better hurry and get paint on the raw wood before winter.

I lifted my hand to knock when the front door flew open.

"Oh," Luke said when he saw me. "You're not the pizza guy." He peered past me as if the pizza man would appear behind me.

"No, I'm not. I…"

"Get in here. It's getting cold out there." He pulled me through the door, then turned and walked toward the back of the house. He was wearing a pair of jeans, a soft-looking crew-neck T-shirt, and socks. He looked extremely comfortable, as if he was in for the night.

I stared after him, wondering if I should follow.

"I thought you said you had plans," he said. He turned and realized I hadn't followed. "What's wrong?"

How did I tell him that I was no good at this? That I hadn't had a male friend in a really long time? Casual flings, yes, but… Wait a minute. That's all this had the potential to be. Why was I making it anything more than that?

I gave my head a little shake. "Nothing. I was just... My plans were canceled. And I thought..." I was stumbling over my words.

He pretended not to notice. He raised the beer bottle in his hand. "Want one?"

I nodded. "Come on then. Cooper went to get more. I ordered pizza. You hungry?"

"I suppose?"

I followed him to the kitchen, and he handed me a beer from the fridge. Then he stepped closer and brushed his cool fingers along my cheekbone. "Doesn't look like you'll bruise too badly."

I looked around. "I'd heard that Coop was fixing up the place. I like the changes he's made so far." I walked over to the back windows. I couldn't see much in the dark, but I knew our homes were separated by about five acres. "It's a big house for one person."

"I'm sure he's hoping that he's not always on his own here. Or maybe he'll fix it up and flip it."

I faced him again. "Either of those scenarios makes sense."

"Did you come by for a reason? And 'just to see me' is an acceptable answer." He grinned. He didn't act like a serious FBI agent when he was away from work. He was relaxed and seemed easy-going, like someone I would enjoy hanging out with—if I were the hanging-out type.

I didn't answer his question. Instead I asked, "Why did you ask Matthew Lake if he knew the victims of the Midland fire?"

Luke took another drink of his beer while considering. When he didn't answer, only stared at me, I continued. "You actually think you have a serial arsonist." I lifted a finger. "Worse—you think you have a serial killer on your hands. If it were just an arsonist, he'd just be setting fires. This person is killing his victims before setting the fires."

Just considering the possibility stirred up a rush of memories. Unable to control those visions, I stumbled backwards a little, and reached out for the kitchen island to steady myself.

"Whoa!" Luke said. He set his beer down and rushed over to me, placing a hand on my arm. "You okay?" He took the bottle from my hand. "Come sit." He led me over to a stool on the other side of the island.

"Sorry," I said. "I just got a little light-headed. I haven't eaten much today." That was a lie, of course. I stared straight ahead at a spot on the granite countertop—a new addition to the house, if I had to guess. "You don't really think Matthew killed the Siegelmans or the Reynoldses. You as much as said that." I was processing my thoughts, attempting to guess at the deductive reasoning Luke was using. I refocused on his eyes. "Questioning Matthew Lake was just ruling him out."

Luke said nothing. He was just letting me talk.

Another thought popped into my head. "Why haven't you pulled Ethan in for questioning?"

"We're watching him."

"Were you watching him already the night of the Reynolds fire?"

"No. We had to jump through some hoops first. The Reynolds fire helped me get the permission."

I pressed my fingers into my forehead. "And that's why you came here to Paynes Creek." This was getting out of control. Why didn't Ethan go somewhere else? Why couldn't he have just settled in a town or state far away from here?

"I came to Paynes Creek because you had a murder

that resembled at least two other cases I was investigating. I don't know if they're related yet."

"But you think they are."

The sound of the front door opening had me jumping off the barstool. Luke was standing close, and his hand went to my waist.

Coop's voice preceded him. "Pizza, beer, and football. Is there anything bet—" He stepped into the kitchen and stopped short. "Oh, you have company." His grin spread all the way to his eyes.

"I should go," I said quickly. I pressed a hand into Luke's chest to push him aside, but he didn't budge.

"No. Have pizza with us." Luke turned. "Coop, you know—"

"Faith Day. Of course." He stepped forward and held out a hand.

I stepped around Luke, thankful that he dropped his hand, and shook Coop's hand. "Good to see you, Cooper."

"You like football?" he asked, eyeing his friend, then returning his gaze to me.

"Yes, but I…"

"Then it's settled. You a Cowboys or Steelers fan? 'Cause that's who's playing."

"Browns, actually."

"Okay. Okay. I can live with that. You can stay." Coop nodded, obviously teasing me. "I'll get plates and napkins. Luke, get us all more beer." Coop walked to the other side of the kitchen and began pulling dishes from a cabinet.

Luke turned to me. "You alright? We can leave if you'd like to talk more."

I angled my head. "Why would you leave? I'm the one who barged in on your guys' night."

"There wouldn't be a guys' night had you not rejected me earlier."

"He's right," Coop said. "I thought I saw a tear."

Luke made a pouty face.

"You're mocking me," I said. There was no humor in my voice, and I immediately regretted it. I just wasn't the type of flirtatious girl these two were probably used to. And this investigation was invading my personal space a little too much. "Look, I appreciate the invite. But I really need to go." I started for the hall, adding a quick, "It was good to see you, Cooper" as I went.

I'd made it to the front door before Luke caught up to me. "What just happened back there?"

"Nothing. I'm just not interested in staying for pizza." Or whatever else was going on between Luke and me.

He placed his hand on the door. "Look, I think you're interested in me. And I'm definitely interested in you. I know Ethan is a tough subject for you. We don't have to talk about him. Not tonight." He paused a long second. "Did I get a completely wrong signal from you?"

My pulse sped up, and I drilled the heel of my palm into the spot over my heart. I looked up at Luke, unable to hide the distress I was feeling. "I'm sorry. I just can't."

"Hey," he said. He removed his hand from the door and cupped my cheek. "This has to do with way more than what happened here tonight, right? What's got you so worked up?"

With his hand gone from the door, I pulled it open, ducked away from his touch, and fled before I had to answer his question.

By the time I climbed into my car, I felt utterly foolish. But I couldn't do anything about it. Luke was right about one thing. There was some sort of attraction between us. The part that he got wrong was my willingness to do anything about it.

THIRTEEN

The night was still young, I was still hungry, and I didn't want to go home. So I called Aubrey.

"You guys home?" I asked when she answered.

"I'm here. Just got home from my Pistol Packin' Mamas meeting."

I chuckled. Aubrey was part of a shooting club with other women, mostly friends from church. They got together once a month to practice shooting their firearms, then went out for drinks after. Sometimes they even went out of town for weekend shooting retreats. She had tried to get me involved, but group activities just weren't my thing.

"You're home early," I said.

"Yeah, since I can't drink, I came on home. But it's just me—Finch got called in for an emergency surgery on a cat." She sighed. "You looking for dinner? I've got leftover lasagna. And a bottle of wine I bought but can't enjoy thanks to this two-pound alien I'm growing."

"I'd be happy to enjoy your wine and cooking. On my way."

I drove through town toward their house. Just as I was

about to turn into their neighborhood, a combination of sirens blared from somewhere behind me. In my rearview mirror, I saw a fire truck turn the corner and head straight for me. I pulled over and let the vehicle pass. Directly behind the fire truck was Uncle Henry in his red pickup truck, his red lights flashing up a fury, and before I could pull back out onto the road, two more vehicles—a Paynes Creek PD squad car and an ambulance—raced in from a different direction, passing through the intersection directly in front of me.

When I saw fire, police, and ambulance, I normally would assume they were headed for a bad car accident, but because they were going into a neighborhood, my mind jumped to a different conclusion. I decided to follow. I had my camera equipment in the back; I might be of some use.

The lights flickered behind homes and trees, and as I neared, I could see a gray smoke billowing into the night sky.

When I turned the corner on the last street in the back of the neighborhood—the street where Finch and Aubrey lived—I saw the flames shooting up and out from one of the homes. I was relieved to see it wasn't Finch's. But it was still Paynes Creek's second devastating fire in less than a week.

I parked and got out, grabbing my coat and camera bag from the back seat. When I approached the police cars that were already positioned as a barricade, one of the uniforms lifted his chin in my direction. "Hi, Faith. They called you in quickly."

I walked past him, giving him a nod.

Neighbors had gathered on the sidewalk across the street to watch. The firefighters had hooked up a hose to the fire hydrant and were spraying water to the second story. Other firefighters were fighting the lower-level flames with water from the truck. And I spotted my uncle close to the house, giving orders to one of the younger firefighters.

And then I saw something unexpected: Luke Justice. He was still in jeans, but had added a dark green barn jacket. He arrived with Chief Reid, and they were walking toward the ambulance, where EMTs appeared to be performing CPR on someone. Luke must have received the call right after I left Coop's.

The EMT stopped his CPR, looked at his watch, then backed away from the gurney. Chief Reid shook his head.

Luke then spotted me. He said something to the chief, the chief nodded, looking in my direction, and Luke walked toward me.

"Hey," he said. A casual hello, as if I hadn't just run away from him. "Can you get photos of the crowd?"

"What?" I started to ask why, but then understanding set in. He was thinking that this fire might be arson, and he wondered if the person responsible was here to admire his or her handiwork. It was only then that I recognized whose house was on fire: this was the home of Sadie Porter, another teenage girl linked to Matthew Lake. "Of course," I said.

"Be discreet," he warned. He had kind eyes—the type that told me he truly cared about the victims of his crimes, which didn't help me in my vow to stay away from him. Their forest green color, the same color as his jacket, simply pulled you in and made you want to stay a while.

I nodded. I wanted to ask who had died moments earlier, and if anyone else had been found inside the home, but I assumed I'd know soon enough.

Armed with my camera and a powerful telephoto lens, I stayed to the outer perimeter of the taped-off area without getting close to where the nosy and concerned neighbors gathered. I snapped pictures and made mental notes of anyone I recognized, changing angles and locations from time to time.

"Do they know what happened?" a familiar voice asked behind me.

"Thought you were off saving a cat," I said to Finch without looking at him. I continued snapping photos.

"Mission accomplished. She's in recovery. Is everyone okay? What happened?"

I lowered my camera and looked at him. "No. EMTs were working on one victim, but it looked like they were unsuccessful."

"What? Was it one of the Porters?"

I shrugged. "No one has said."

"Anyone else?"

"Don't know that either."

"Well, I'll make sure the church knows so that they can add the Porters and their family and friends to the prayer list."

"Look around. I'm sure the church already knows." I glanced at Mrs. Kenney, who was standing with her long-time friend, Mrs. Tate, the widow of Mayor Tate, who had died just last year. He hadn't actually been mayor in ten years, but everyone still called him Mayor Tate. Nothing happened in this town that Mrs. Kenney and Mrs. Tate weren't aware of.

"True. Doesn't take long for news to spread in this town."

I spotted Luke again. He was speaking to Uncle Henry, but as if he knew I was staring at him, he looked up at me.

I turned to Finch. "I was actually on my way to your house to bum dinner off of Aubrey when the first responders sped past me."

"Have you eaten?" he asked.

"Not yet."

"Well, come on back to the house."

"I'll meet you there if I finish here soon."

"What, exactly, are you doing?"

"Capturing the faces of the spectators."

"You think someone set the fire on purpose? And that they're still here?"

"Always a possibility," I said with a shrug.

When Finch was gone, I turned toward Luke again, but he had moved. I scanned the area, looking for him, and examined the crowd one last time. It had thinned, but a line of gawkers still stood just beyond the police tape.

That's when I saw him.

Ethan.

He was standing behind a small cluster of women, his face shadowed by a baseball cap. I couldn't see his eyes or make out what he was looking at, but it was definitely him.

I didn't want to believe he might have started these fires. But why else would he risk being here?

I slipped behind a police car and made my way toward him, weaving my way through the remaining people. But Marla Manfield stepped in my path.

"Faith Day, we meet again." She blocked my view of Ethan. "Any idea what started the fire? Is it another case of arson? Do you know who lived here?"

My face hardened at her questions. Did she realize how cold she sounded?

"Marla, I know you're smart enough to figure out that I know as much as you do at this time, and that even if I knew more I'm not in a position to reveal that information to you." I pushed her aside and stretched my neck to spot Ethan again.

But by the time I'd gotten to where I had seen him, he was gone. I spun three hundred sixty degrees, but didn't spot him.

Had he seen me and left? Had he seen Marla corner me?

I let out a long breath, remembering the morning when Ethan visited me in the hospital, right after our own house fire. I closed my eyes, attempting to squash the avalanche of memories, but it was no use.

FOURTEEN

I stared up at the white, tiled ceiling. The hospital room was dark. Machines beeped to my left. I tried to turn my head, but something stopped me. I moaned in pain, but hardly a sound came out. Tears ran down my face.

"You're awake." Ethan's voice, on my right, whispering. "Don't move. I'll get a nurse."

Ethan ran from the room and returned with a nurse on his heels. "Hi, Faith. My name is Dalia. Can you tell me on a scale of one to ten how much pain you're in? With ten being unbearable."

I couldn't even answer her. I just burst into tears. "Is my mom dead?" I asked. I wanted to hear someone say what I already knew to be true. I knew she'd been in the house—that was why I ran in to save her. And I saw her there, on the floor of the kitchen, flames all around her. I knelt beside her, pleaded with her to wake up. And I didn't care that the flames were consuming the room and leaping onto my clothes. Just when I decided I didn't care what happened to me and that I wasn't leaving my mother, arms circled around me and pulled me backward.

Ethan's arms.

He laid me on the ground outside the house. He put out the flames, patting me down with his bare hands and then with the shirt off of his own back.

"Sweetie," Dalia said. She stroked the hair on the right side of my head. "Your mama died in the fire last night. I'm so sorry."

I squeezed my eyes tight, sobbing silent cries due to a throat trashed by smoke inhalation.

Ethan stepped up behind Dalia. She glanced at him, then back at me. "I'll give you two a minute while I go call the doctor and let him know you're awake. Also, the police want to talk to you, and the fire chief has been calling constantly."

When Dalia had left, Ethan sat in a chair beside me. He scooped up my right hand and leaned his head against our clasped palms. "I am so sorry, Faith. Can you ever forgive me?"

I stared at the top of his head, at his sandy-blond hair darkened from soot. Then I took in the left side of my body. Bandages covered my left arm. I was wearing a hospital gown, but I could feel the bandages reaching all the way up my neck. I wanted to ask Ethan how bad my injuries were. No—I wanted the nurse to come back so that I could ask her.

Ethan lifted his head. "I didn't mean to hurt you," he said. "I'm so sorry." Tears touched his eyes. "Tell me what I can do to make this better."

I blinked away my own tears. For the briefest of moments, I pushed away the vivid image of my mom and Eli lying dead on the kitchen floor. I met Ethan's devastated expression. His face conveyed all the pain and heartbreak of a seventeen-year-old who had just lost his father —and he *did* look genuinely sorry.

"Get out," I said softly.

Tears fell from his eyes. "You don't mean that. You have to forgive me. You're all I have now."

"I never want to see you again." I forced the words out louder this time, burning my throat with each syllable.

Ethan dropped my hand and stood. "Don't push me away, Faith. You need me. We need each other. We both lost everything last night."

"I lost more," I whispered, and I closed my eyes.

FIFTEEN

When I was sure there was nothing more I could do at the scene, I took my camera and climbed into my car. I had lost my appetite, so I texted Finch and Aubrey to let them know I wouldn't be stopping by.

Instead, I continued through town, compelled to drive down memory lane, past the spots where Ethan and I would hang out with friends during high school—mostly the parking lots of fast food restaurants. They were the highlights of many of our Friday and Saturday nights. I then drove through the parking lot of the library and over to the city park. I angled my SUV to shine the headlights on the swings where Ethan and I sat many afternoons, talking for hours. Tonight, the swings squeaked in the wind.

I leaned my head into the steering wheel. "What are you doing?" I asked myself. "Was Ethan even there tonight?" I had almost convinced myself that I had imagined him.

But I wasn't crazy. He was definitely there.

I backed out of the parking spot and headed home.

My trailer was dark when I pulled onto the long drive, but as I neared, I spotted a vehicle parked in the turn-around spot. Luke's vehicle.

I grabbed my camera bag—I would digitally process the photos first thing in the morning—and approached my trailer slowly.

"What are you doing here?" I asked.

Luke was sitting in one of the Adirondack chairs on my front porch, which was basically a low wooden deck. His hair was wet, and he was wearing different clothes and a different jacket.

"Waiting for you." He stuffed his hands in his pockets and shivered.

"Why?"

"Because I'm hoping you'll reconsider your stance on pushing me away."

His face had that expression I see sometimes on detectives when a case hits them a little too deeply. "You want a drink?" I walked past him and stuck a key in the door.

He pushed himself up from the chair and stood behind me—so close I could feel his breath on the back of my neck. "No," he said in a low, husky voice.

The muscles in my spine tensed. I dropped my hand slowly and turned. Looking up into his dark eyes, I realized I was powerless against whatever was happening between us—lust, passion, my need for someone to understand the memories that these fires were dredging up.

"Don't tell me to leave," he said. "I'll leave if you tell me to. But please don't."

I stepped closer to him. I stared at his chest for a moment. Thinking. Processing consequences. He didn't move.

I knew, as did he, that whatever happened would go no further than the length of this case—if it even went beyond this single night—which meant he could be using me. Or vice versa.

And that was okay. I could use him to add a memorable night to my memory collection. And maybe a good memory would help make one of the bad fade.

If only that were how my hyperthymesia worked.

Luke just stood there. Waiting for me to say something. Or do something.

I lifted my head. When our eyes locked, I didn't have to say a word. He reached for my shoulder and lifted the heavy camera bag from it. His gaze burned into me; I could feel the heat all the way in the pit of my stomach. I turned and led him inside.

As he set the camera bag on my dining table, I shrugged out of my jacket.

"I reek of smoke," I said.

"I don't care." He stepped toward me.

I lifted a hand to stop him from getting too close. "I'm going to shower. If neither of us has changed our mind by the time I get out, you can stay."

The look in his eyes told me it would not be he who changed his mind.

A divider separated my bedroom, the bathroom, and my closet from the rest of the Airstream. I passed through and shut it behind me. Gus was stretched out across the middle of my bed and barely lifted her head when I entered.

"What am I doing?" I asked her.

She answered by stretching her front paws and then burrowing further into my down comforter.

I covered my face with my hands and raked them over my skin. Then I ripped my clothes off and went to the shower. Maybe some cool water would wake me up to what a colossal mistake I was about to make.

When I'd scrubbed the smoke smell from my hair and body, I got out of the shower, ran a brush through my hair, and grabbed the most unsexy T-shirt and sweatpants I could find in my closet.

I returned to the living area to find Luke flipping through the *Paynes Creek Gazette*, the local newspaper. For a small town, they did a good job of covering everything: political news, human interest stories, sports, and of course, the most-read section of any small-town paper: the weekly crime reports.

Luke didn't look up, though he obviously knew I was there. "Did you know that Dick Taylor had twelve dollars worth of gas plus a gas can stolen out of his garage last week?"

The crime reports weren't *supposed* to be comical, but they often were.

"Not sure why anyone would want to live in this crime-infested town," I said.

Luke put down the paper and looked at me. *Analyzed* me was more like it. I suddenly regretted my choice in clothing. He slid out from the booth at my table, keeping his eyes on me.

"You probably should have left," I said weakly.

He stalked toward me. "I didn't want to leave." When he reached me, he didn't touch me. He just stood there, looking down into my eyes.

I sensed he was seeing straight through me with his investigative mind. Did he know I was hiding things from him—things that might impact the direction of his inquiry? Things I'd never told a single soul? Would he still be standing here, looking at me like he wished I hadn't bothered with any clothes at all, if he knew the baggage I carried—or that my silence might have helped an innocent man go to prison?

"Luke," I said. "There's something—"

In one motion, he slid a hand around my waist, planting it firmly in the small of my back, while placing his opposite fingers over my lips. "I know these circumstances aren't ideal. I'm sure I'm breaking all sorts of professional and ethical rules. But for some reason, I don't care."

I think he knew the instant I let my gaze travel from his eyes to his lips that I, too, was ready to block out all possible objections to us being present in this moment.

His mouth captured mine in a demanding, brutal kiss. We stayed like that for several beats before he pulled back slightly, almost as if he'd thought better of the aggressive way he'd attacked.

I arched into him, letting him know it was okay—that I wasn't fragile. I could feel the way his body reacted instantly. He backed me toward my room.

I broke the kiss long enough to whisper against his lips, "I'll get a call to be back at the scene at dawn."

"That's tomorrow. I'm only concerned with right now. With you." His lips nipped and bit along my jaw to my neck, kissing and sucking as he went. "God, you taste and smell amazing."

He lifted me, allowing me to wrap my legs around his waist. My hands dove into his hair as I kissed him.

Gus growled when we got closer to the bed. Just before Luke deposited me onto the queen-size mattress, she hissed and leapt out of the way.

"I think I made your cat angry."

"You can make it up to her later," I said. On my knees on the bed, I unbuttoned his shirt, staring at his chest. I was suddenly nervous.

He crooked a finger under my chin and lifted my face. "There will be another time for this slow, seductive undressing you've got going. Right now? I want you too badly to wait."

He reached down and grabbed the hem of my shirt.

I latched on to his hand and stopped him, suddenly feeling the need to warn him about what the fire had done to me so many years ago. "Luke," I said softly. "I have scars."

He drew back, finished taking his shirt off, and let it drop to the floor. "So do I." He pointed to a scar just below his left breast, and another in his right shoulder.

"You were shot?" I lifted my eyes to meet his.

"Twice, apparently. I have emotional scars, too, but I'll save those for another day."

I framed his face with my hands and kissed him. Then I kissed each of his scars. "I'm sorry someone hurt you."

He looked at me then. Really looked at me. "I knew almost the instant we met that this was going to be a complicated relationship."

I wasn't sure what he meant, and I didn't care. I lifted my shirt up and off.

Luke ran his fingers along the scars that were left behind after the most important night of my life. His skin was cool, and in the wake of his touch, he left a trail of goose bumps. His fingers brushed up my neck.

"I think you're beautiful," he said, his eyes glued to mine.

And that was it. I threw my arms around his neck. He crushed his lips to mine. And we lost ourselves in each other, blocking out everything happening outside of that small space we found ourselves in.

I saw the flicker of light behind my eyelids before it registered. Then I opened my eyes, and I knew: it had happened again.

I heard the subtle click of the trailer door. I scrambled from the bed and ran to the other end of the trailer.

"Faith?" Luke stirred behind me. He must have seen how fast I was moving. "What's wrong?"

I flew out of the trailer and ran toward the bonfire, already raging. I wasn't sure if Luke had brought out this fearlessness in me, seeing as I was terrified when this happened a few nights ago, or if I was finally just pissed off enough that I didn't care.

"Ethan!" I yelled. "If that's you... so help me." So help me what, exactly? How could I possibly threaten him?

Luke came running out of the trailer with his pants on and no shirt. His gun was drawn.

"What the hell is this?" he asked, stopping beside me.

"Apparently, this is my wakeup call after house fires now." I turned and stormed back inside.

Luke stayed outside for another ten minutes, checking the area. When he finally returned, he confirmed what I already knew. "Whoever was here is gone now." He rubbed his face, drilling fingers into his eyelids. "How many times has this happened?"

I had already blown out the lit candles around the trailer. "Three times, each one right after a house fire— the two here in Paynes Creek and the one over in Midland."

"Wait a minute. What about the candles? Did you light those?"

I gave my head a little shake, looking away from Luke. I was wearing nothing but a T-shirt and panties, and suddenly I felt bashful—and cold—so I went to my bedroom and grabbed a pair of jeans.

"You're telling me that you called *this* in to the police?

That someone had broken into your home and lit candles, and those assholes didn't believe you?"

I looked up at him, holding my jeans in front of me. "The first time this happened, and the only time I called it in, it was only a fire in the pit and a bouquet of daisies on my bed. It was the next time that the person came in and lit candles."

"What's significant about daisies?"

I looked away.

"Faith?" he prompted. "You called out to Ethan. Do you think he's doing this? Why would he leave you daisies?"

"He's the only one who's ever known that my favorite flower is the daisy. My mother used to tell me that 'daisy' was the first word I ever said. I thought every flower was a daisy, so I said it a lot. Ethan would bring me daisies for my birthday, or when I had bad days."

"He's the only one?"

"Well, my mom used to put daisies in my room on special occasions." I swiped at my cheek where a stray tear had fallen. "I'm sorry. I…" How did I tell Luke that I remembered everything like it had just happened? Specific details of every day, no matter how many years ago, were embedded in my memory like they occurred ten minutes ago.

He ran a hand through his hair. "The chief better have an incredible explanation for not taking you more seriously."

I closed the distance between us, slipped my hand into his, and forced him to look at me. "You can't say anything."

"Why the fuck not?" He was angry, which I didn't understand. Why did he care *that* much?

I pulled my hand away and straightened. "Because this

isn't your problem. And saying something will only make my life harder." I turned and headed back to the bedroom. The sun was starting to rise, and I knew I would get a call from the station any minute telling me to get over to the Porter house.

Luke caught up to me. "What just happened?"

I shimmied into my jeans and grabbed a bra and sweater. I tried to squeeze past Luke to the bathroom, but he grabbed both shoulders and held me in front of him.

"Talk to me, Faith. Do you truly think Ethan is sneaking into your trailer? To what? Scare you?"

"I don't know," I said quickly. I pressed fingers into my forehead where a headache was forming. "Ethan knows better than to come out here and start a fire. He knows he'd be the first person everyone would look to. But who else?"

"I don't know. But you *need* to report these incidents. The fact that they've occurred after the three fires has to be significant."

I didn't say anything. I didn't have to. Both of our phones rang, within seconds of each other, interrupting our conversation. Mine was from Penelope, calling me in, as I'd expected. Luke's message, I assumed, was similar, as he said, "I'll be right there."

As I finished dressing and slipped into a down jacket, he slid his government-issued Glock into a holster and secured it to his body. Then he stalked toward me and placed a hand on my cheek.

"You have no idea how sorry I am for the way we were awakened this morning. I had an idea for a much better wake-up call." He leaned in and placed a gentle kiss on my lips. "It had to do with you and me, naked in that very comfortable bed of yours." His tone carried a lightness I needed in that moment, but his eyes had something else in them. Pity? Fear? I wasn't sure, but I didn't need either of those emotions weighing me down.

"Luke," I started, but he placed two fingers on my lips.

"If you're going to try to brush me off, don't bother. I don't do one-night stands. Something has happened between us. We'll see it through."

SIXTEEN

I turned sixteen the summer before my junior year. Mom invited everyone over for dinner. Finch had been taking summer classes, but was home on a weeklong break. Uncle Henry and Aunt Leah were there, too.

Eli and Mom surprised Ethan and me with a car—a used Volkswagen sedan in white—that we would share. They couldn't afford the insurance on two vehicles with two sixteen-year-olds in the house, and since Ethan and I pretty much just went to school and back every day, it made sense. On days I stayed after school, he would come back and get me, and on days when he had baseball practice, I would pick him up—after I got my license, of course —or he would catch a ride home with a friend.

After dinner on my birthday, everyone was just sitting around, laughing and eating cake, when Ethan said to me, "How 'bout we take our new car for a spin?"

I looked around at the happy faces all around the table —my entire family in one spot, content. It would be one of the last memories I would have of the entire family together.

"We should help Mom clean up, first," I said.

"What?" Mom laughed and waved us off. "You two go. Have fun! I've got Finch here to help me."

They all laughed at that.

I smiled at Ethan. "Are you going to let me drive?"

Mom yelled, "Absolutely not! You don't even have your permit yet."

But Ethan and I were already running for the door.

What Mom and Eli didn't know—and they would be furious if they did—was that Ethan had been letting me drive in empty parking lots ever since he got his license a few months earlier. He'd been taking every opportunity to drive Mom's or Eli's cars, and I'd taken every opportunity to get my turn at the wheel as well.

Now, as we drove through town in our new-to-us car, we felt giddy with the newfound freedom that only a first car can bring.

"I have a surprise for you," Ethan said.

I smiled. "I'm not sure I can handle any more surprises." I ran my hands over the dashboard and along the seats. "We have our own car."

He reached over, grabbed my hand, brought it to his mouth, and kissed my knuckles.

I didn't think much of it at the time. Ethan loved me. I knew this. And I loved him... as a brother.

He turned in to the school parking lot. It was empty, of course, seeing as it was almost nine o'clock at night.

"Where are we going?" I asked.

"You'll see."

He drove up the hill to the parking lot normally reserved for teachers and seniors. It was also a popular spot for kids to park and/or drink. But it was empty tonight, and with the sun descending and nearly gone behind the trees, the parking lot was heavily shaded and quickly turning dark.

Ethan parked the car and shut off the engine.

"If we get caught up here," I started.

"We're not going to get busted," he said, climbing out of the car. He skirted around the hood, opened my door, and held out a hand. "Besides, we're not doing anything wrong."

He pulled me out, then dropped my hand. He went around to the trunk and pulled out a tote bag and some kind of film projector.

"Wait a minute," I said. "I thought the car was a surprise to the both of us. How is it that you have stuff in the trunk?"

"Actually, I helped pick the car out. I've known about it for weeks."

"And you picked a white car?"

"Well, I was limited in choices, and I thought you would like it."

"I do, but you don't."

"Well, it's not just my car." He lifted his head, urging me to follow. "Come on."

"I still don't understand what we're doing."

"Patience, grasshopper!" he called back.

Ethan spread a blanket on a patch of grass behind the building, then pulled his laptop from the bag and hooked it up to the projector. When he turned it on, my all-time favorite movie—*Breakfast at Tiffany's*—started playing on the side of the white-walled building.

Ethan ran back to the car and got one more thing. He returned and presented me with a bouquet of white daisies. "For you."

"They're beautiful."

"Come on. Sit. I brought loads of theater candy, popcorn, and a couple of sodas to wash it down with."

"You thought of everything."

Ethan and I spent the next two hours watching the movie. Well, Ethan mostly made fun of the movie, and I mostly swooned. We ate copious quantities of junk food, and that was on top of the birthday dinner and cake we'd already eaten. And when it was over, we lay there under the stars and talked until our curfew approached.

"Thank you for making my birthday perfect," I said as I stared up into the night sky.

He rolled onto his side. "You're my best friend. I would do anything for you."

"I know," I said without turning to look at him.

"Faith." His fingers brushed the skin from my shoulder to my elbow. "Do you ever wonder if we would have been close if our parents hadn't… you know… gotten married?"

"Of course we would have. We were friends before our parents even met." We'd talked about this before, but I'd avoided the subject ever since that day on the swings in the park. Ethan had seemed to want to avoid it, too. He'd even had girlfriends since then. Nothing serious, but still.

"Will you let me kiss you?" he asked.

I turned my head to face him. My eyes were adjusted to the darkness, and it was a clear night, so I could see well enough to recognize how he was looking at me. I'd never been kissed by a boy before, so this definitely took me by surprise.

I sat up and looked straight ahead.

He sat up next to me, staring at my profile.

My breathing picked up as I considered what a kiss from him would mean. We were siblings… but we weren't related by blood. And I knew there was an attraction between us. My mother had seen it too—which was why she had made me promise, long ago, that Ethan and I would always be siblings and nothing more.

But now, as I turned my head to look at him—my best friend, a person I'd trust with my life—I wondered what it would be like to kiss a boy on my sixteenth birthday. A boy who I knew loved me and would never hurt me.

"If we do this…" I said. "It's a one-time thing."

His face brightened. "Agreed." His lips twitched, but he didn't move.

"No one can ever know. This has to stay between us."

He leaned toward me and slipped a hand around my neck. "I would never hurt you, Faith. I want to be the first one to kiss you, so that you'll know what it's like to be kissed by someone who loves you. I don't want you to ever settle for anything less."

When I thought about his words later, they sounded so grown-up. Even in that moment, they were perfect—and exactly what I wanted to hear.

He kissed me. It was soft at first. Then something ignited deep inside my gut. I reached a hand out and steadied myself by holding on to his arm. He deepened the kiss and pushed me back onto the blanket.

We made out for more than thirty minutes. We got swept up in a mess of hormones, attraction, and mutual trust. And when his hand lingered along the side of my body, caressing my breast, I didn't stop him.

Not until it struck me how late it was.

I pushed him off of me. "Shit, Ethan. The time."

I jumped up and started stuffing our trash and supplies into the tote bag.

Ethan laughed. "It'll be fine. They know we're out together."

I stopped what I was doing and stared at him. "What

have we done?" I asked. I touched my swollen lips, then proceeded to smooth out my hair.

He stood and grabbed my hand. "Nothing that shouldn't have happened. It's been a long time coming. Surely you felt that. The connection we have comes along once in a lifetime."

I didn't move. My eyes were fixed on his. I was holding the tote in my hand. "Ethan, we can't. This can't happen."

"Maybe not now."

I stepped back. "Not ever. I told you. I trusted you."

"Okay," he said, sounding panicked. "We'll do this your way. You trusted me. It won't happen again."

I nodded.

"You're my best friend, Faith. I won't do anything to jeopardize that."

But he did. Not immediately, but eventually. He broke his promise.

And after that, everything between us was ruined.

SEVENTEEN

I scrolled through the photographs of the latest Paynes Creek arson case on my laptop. Just as in the Reynolds fire, a married couple—in this case, the parents of Sadie Porter—was found dead inside. And as in the Reynolds case, the couple was already dead before the fire even started—at least, according to the message I received from Luke.

But unlike the Reynolds fire, in this fire there was another victim: Sadie Porter. She was the one the paramedics had been trying to resuscitate when I arrived on the scene. Multiple eyewitnesses had stated that Sadie ran into the fire in an attempt to save her parents, and the burns she received were too much for her body to handle. Even if the paramedics had managed to keep her breathing, she would have been looking at a long, painful recovery.

I digitally touched up my photos, making sure what I sent the investigators was clear, bright enough, and in focus —but without altering them in any material way. Then I uploaded the lot of them onto a secure server that the

Paynes Creek PD and other law enforcement agencies could access.

With my official duties complete, I scrolled through the photos again—this time for my own purposes. I went back through the photos of the crowd until I found Ethan. Or... maybe Ethan. The man's baseball cap shielded his face, so I couldn't be sure.

But if it *was* him, why was he being so stupid? He'd managed to learn the law while in prison, becoming what many referred to as a jailhouse lawyer. And he'd somehow landed a job despite everyone around here knowing him as the kid who killed his father and stepmother. Why would he jeopardize that?

Unless he truly is a psychopath.

That was what Luke believed—or so I suspected. The truth was, he'd told me little about his theories. All I knew for sure was that he'd come to Paynes Creek to take a look at the Reynolds fire, had asked an awful lot of questions about my mom's case... and had gotten awfully close to me in a very short time.

AT SEVEN P.M. I filled Gus's food bowl, gave her a little scratch behind the ears, and grabbed my coat. Penelope's son had recovered from his fever, and she had agreed to meet me for dinner at Boone's Taphouse.

I stepped outside and held my coat tightly around me. The temperature had dropped quite a bit, and I'd heard that Kentucky might see a rare October snowstorm. I walked to my car and was just reaching in my pocket to pull out my keys when someone cleared their throat behind me.

I spun around.

Ethan took a step back with his hands out to the sides. "Hi, Faith."

I held my keys so as to form a sharp weapon between my fisted fingers. "What are you doing here? You know this is really stupid."

"I needed to see you. To make sure you're alright."

"Why?" I asked, while calculating how quickly I could unlock the door, get in the driver's seat, and speed off.

He took a step toward me. I instinctively backed away.

"Come on, Faith. You know me. I'm not here to hurt you. Deep down, I know you remember me. Who I was. Who I am. The friendship we had."

I studied him again. "Did they brainwash you in prison?"

"Prison changes a person—that's for sure. But deep down, I'm still the same person. Isn't that what you came to find out the other night?"

I shifted on my feet. My eyes darted from him to my vehicle. I didn't want him thinking I had come looking for him at the Spotted Cat.

When I didn't answer, he seemed to deflate. "Are you really scared of me?"

"What did you expect, Ethan?" So many memories washed over me. I remembered the day we met. I remembered the many hours we'd spent together—watching movies, playing video games, or just hanging out. I remembered the day our parents told us they were getting married, the wedding, and the many holidays we'd subsequently spent together as brother and sister.

And I remembered when it all changed—when *he* changed things between us.

"You know I never meant to hurt you." He paused, looked up into the sky—at what, I had no idea—then back at me. "I was drunk that night. You were, too. And you've spent the past twelve years changing the facts of that night inside your mind."

That's where he was wrong. It wasn't possible for me to change the facts in my mind. God, I wished I could.

Finding courage from somewhere deep inside me, I took a step forward and stuck a finger in his face. "Drunk is no excuse for what you did to me. No amount of time will change that."

"Did I deserve to go to prison for what I did?" His voice rose. "I was sentenced to *life*. Hell, at the time, I felt like I'd received the death penalty—for a crime I didn't commit! And you *let* them do it to me."

"You killed our parents," I said through gritted teeth.

Instead of fighting back … instead of coming at me with more excuses about his drunken state the night of the fire… he slowly slipped his hands into his coat pockets. His face softened, and he lowered his voice. "You know I didn't."

"How could I possibly know such a thing?" I asked, but there was very little energy behind the question.

"Now look who's been brainwashed," he said sarcastically. "Who finally convinced you? Your Uncle Henry? Your brother? Or no… let me guess… Chief Reid laid out the evidence. Somehow he convinced you that I was capable of killing both my father and your mother, then burning down our house." His tone was mocking. "Oh, and let's not forget… then I spotted you running into the flames, and upon having a miraculous reversal of conscience or morals or whatever, I ran in after you to save your life."

I didn't say anything. I couldn't. I couldn't stop how fresh the memories of his arms around me were. Pulling me from the burning and collapsing house. Our teenage years going up in flames along with our parents' bodies.

"Isn't that what my poor excuse for an attorney said in the sentencing phase of the trial?" he continued. "That since I'd saved your life, the judge should have mercy on me. He 'saved me from the death penalty.' That's what he told the media—that he saved me." Ethan scoffed.

I just stared at him while I willed my racing heart to slow.

He was right about one thing: Chief Reid, along with my aunt and uncle, *had* laid out the facts in such a way that left me with no question that Ethan was guilty. Even when I told them that Ethan had been with me that night, they came up with a timeline that convinced me it was still possible for Ethan to have killed our parents. They never asked what Ethan and I had been doing, and I didn't tell. Ethan hadn't either, to my knowledge.

If I had, would it have made a difference? Or would it have been worse for him?

No. I shook my head. *I couldn't have helped him.* I'd been over the night's events so many times it made me crazy. I'd been over the facts that Chief Reid and Uncle Henry had shared with me—including the gas cans in his car, which Ethan had never explained. Yes, Ethan had *definitely* had time to commit the murders and set the house on fire before I arrived home.

"I didn't do those horrific things," Ethan said quietly. "You, of all people, must know that. We were best friends, Faith. You knew me."

"I thought I did," I said. Tears stung my eyes and ran down my cheeks. The cold air nearly froze them there.

The truth was, as much as I wanted to hold on to the adults' version of the story, deep down I still harbored some doubt. But I was also still angry. I remembered the way Ethan's hands felt that night. And the way he smelled —the distinct cologne that was popular with teenage boys

126

then. That smell was etched into my mind forever, because he didn't normally wear cologne when he was with me.

But what if I'd been wrong? What if I had let him go to prison for a crime he hadn't actually committed—for the wrong crime? What if I could have stopped it?

That fear had been in the back of my mind since the day the verdict was read. Even when Uncle Henry and Aunt Leah constantly reassured me that Ethan could "no longer hurt me."

"No," I said, shaking my head. "No!" I met his gaze again, feeling stronger. I straightened. The muscles in my neck and shoulders tightened, and my hands formed fists at my sides. "I *thought* I knew you, but I was wrong. What you did to me that night was inexcusable. And whether you went to jail for that or for the fire made no difference to me."

"You don't mean that."

"The hell I don't. Now get off my land."

"Faith…" There was so much hurt in that one word. "I served my time. I did it for you."

What did he mean by that? It didn't matter. "You need to leave, Ethan. If I catch you here again—inside my trailer or on my land—I will do everything I can to send you back to prison."

His eyes narrowed. "Inside your trailer? Why would I—"

"Don't you dare play games with me, Ethan. Don't stand there and act like you haven't been stalking me, lighting my fire pit, coming inside my home. You can't hurt me anymore."

He shook his head. "I haven't. This is the first time I've been here in twelve years. Since that night. I'm not sure I would have come had you not come to the Spotted Cat. Why *did* you go there? And then you just ran away. Why?"

"I only came because you left a Spotted Cat matchbook beside my fire pit. I didn't know for sure it was you who left it until I saw you behind the bar. Look, Ethan. You're out of prison, and there's nothing I can do about that. But you *will* stay away from me. Better yet, stay out of this town. Move on. You've been given a second chance— so take it. And leave me out of it."

He didn't leave—though he did appear to be thinking hard about what I was saying. "I swear I haven't been anywhere near here, Faith. I'm being honest with you. The last thing I would ever do is hurt you. I finally got my life back, and I assumed that life would never include you. And then, there you were, as if in a dream. Standing in my bar."

I swiped at my face. I was so confused. Standing in front of me was the man who had been my best friend for the better part of five years—my impressionable teen years.

But he was also the man who killed my mother.

And the man who raped me the very same night.

EIGHTEEN

Twenty minutes later, I walked into Boone's in a thoroughly dazed and confused state. Luke was there, with Cooper Adams and a couple of off-duty police officers, including Officer Puckett. Luke spotted me immediately and lifted his head in a hello. Cooper gave him a smile and the shake of a head, whatever that meant.

I gave a tight nod in return then looked around and saw Penelope sitting in a booth. I lifted a hand and motioned to her that I would only be a minute.

I approached the table of men. The off-duties eyed me suspiciously.

"Can I talk to you a minute, Special Agent Justice?" I asked. I hugged my arms around me to hide that I was still shaking from the run-in with Ethan.

The others at the table exchanged looks.

"Of course." Luke stood, and with a touch to my arm, he led me to the hallway in the back that led to the bathrooms. "You okay?" He slid his hand down my arm until it touched my hand. "Your hand is freezing." He studied me harder. "And you're shaking. What's wrong?" His eyes widened with concern.

I pulled my hand back and crossed my arms again. "I need to know why you suspect Ethan of setting these fires."

Luke stiffened, looked toward the table of police officers, then back at me. "I never said I suspected Ethan of anything."

A woman stepped out of the bathroom. Instead of backing up so the woman could pass between us, Luke moved in close to me, and the woman walked past behind him.

He placed a hand on my arm again—a reassuring touch. "Let's go somewhere. You can tell me what's going on."

I shrugged away from his touch. "What do you mean? If he's not a suspect, why are you in Paynes Creek? Why are you giving the fires here more attention than the others?"

He managed to keep his face unreadable. "The investigation is ongoing. I'm simply following the trail of evi—"

"Don't give me that rehearsed detective bullshit." I tried to keep my voice at a whisper; the officers were watching us with increased curiosity. "I saw Ethan tonight. He came to the farm."

"What? Did you call someone? Do the police know?"

I shook my head. "We've been over this. The police think I'm crazy. And besides, you just said you weren't actively investigating him."

"That's not what I said. And we have no idea if the fires and your recent break-ins are related. I'm not ruling Ethan out as a person of interest."

"There you go sounding like a detective again."

He took a deep breath. When he spoke again, he sounded calmer. "Did he threaten you?"

I considered the shock I felt when he snuck up behind me, and how his presence at my home made me feel insecure and weak. "Not really."

"You should have called the police. Or someone." He inched closer. "You should have called me immediately. If not to let me help, to let me have a conversation with him."

I lifted my eyes. "You can have a conversation with Ethan anytime you'd like. What I want to know is, why are you in Paynes Creek? Have you discovered something that makes you suspect Ethan in these recent arson cases? And do you think he was released from prison on a technicality or because he truly is innocent?"

"I can't answer any of that."

"Can't, or won't?"

His face softened. "Just because I haven't named Ethan Gentry as a suspect in my investigation doesn't mean I'm not interested in making sure he's fit to be out of prison— if not for my investigation, for your well being. Now, do you want to tell me what Ethan said?"

"I told him about the matchbook from the Spotted Cat. He said he hadn't been to the farm in twelve years."

"So he's claiming he's not the one breaking into your trailer and setting fires in your fire pit."

"That's what he said." I glanced over my shoulder. Penelope was waiting patiently. "Look, I'm meeting someone for dinner."

He narrowed his gaze. "Don't brush me off. Not about this."

"Thanks for listening to me," I deadpanned. I was definitely brushing him off. "I'll be sure to call you if I hear from Ethan again."

I wasn't necessarily lying, but I certainly was questioning the decision to get closer to Luke. He was here for an investigation. That was all.

Before I could rush off, Luke stopped me with a hand to my arm. "I don't know why you just clammed up, but I'll accept it for now. I'm here to help, Faith. If Ethan threatens you in any way, or if you have another break-in, I want to know about it immediately."

I nodded, if only to appease him, before walking over to Penelope's booth. I ignored the table of gawking officers as I passed.

Penelope grinned as I slid into the booth. "You slept with him, didn't you? I know that look between quarreling lovers."

A server arrived at the table. She wore a black T-shirt with the Boone's Taphouse logo across the chest. Her brunette hair, which was cut into a short bob with blonde-dyed tips, was tucked smoothly behind her ears. Pinpoint diamonds sparkled in her ears. "What can I get you, Faith?"

"Hi, Nikki." I looked over at Penelope's pink cosmopolitan and frowned. "Rye Manhattan. With Elkhorn Reserve."

Penelope lifted a single brow. "This *is* serious."

Nikki left to put in my order.

"Did you hear?" Penelope asked. "We're supposed to get a winter storm. Can you believe it? It's been a while since we saw winter this early. It's only October, for crying out loud." Penelope knew me well enough to know when I was having trouble with something, which was why she was going on about the weather. But apparently her curiosity couldn't wait. She set her drink down and pushed it away. "So tell me, what was that about?" She nodded in the direction of Luke.

I lifted a shoulder. "I slept with him." I didn't want to tell her about Ethan. I already regretted mentioning it to Luke.

"I knew it." She leaned closer. "Tell me everything."

"I'll get to that, but first tell me about the Porter fire. Have they linked it to the Reynolds case?"

She leaned back, clearly disappointed I wanted to talk shop first. "If they have, no one's talking yet. Reporters have been sniffing around all day. You remember Marla Manfield?"

"Yeah, she practically attacked me outside the police station the other day. And again last night."

"Well, she's been hanging around asking all sorts of questions. She was at Boone's when I arrived tonight, and she all but cornered Luke out in the parking lot."

"Did you hear what she asked him?"

"Same thing you asked me: Were the two fires connected? And whether the FBI's interest had anything to do with—" Penelope stopped herself abruptly.

"Go on. You can say it."

"Well... she wanted to know if they were linking the fires to Ethan's release from prison." Penelope frowned. "Ah, honey! I'm sorry. I know this brings up all sorts of bad memories for you."

"It's okay," I said, to let her off the hook. "It was a long time ago." Of course, it was like yesterday to me. I could still smell the smoke from the fire, and feel the burns on my skin. I skimmed my fingers over my neck, over the scars that provided a constant reminder—not just to me, but to this town—of what had happened.

Penelope and I decided to share an appetizer, and we each ordered a salad. It wasn't nearly enough food to absorb the cocktails we spent the next two hours drinking. By the time Penelope's husband showed up, we were sloshed.

He flashed an angry scowl in my direction. "Why is it

that whenever my wife meets you for dinner, I have to come retrieve her at some point during the night?"

"Oh, Steven," Penelope slurred while slapping a playful hand at his arm. "Don't blame her. I started drinking before she even got here." She shook her head at me. "Don't mind him. It's past his bedtime."

"Yeah, it is," Steven said. "I have to be at work in a few hours." He helped her up from the booth. She stumbled, but he caught her.

"I'm sorry, Steven," I said sheepishly, but smiled. "I would have been happy to get her home."

He leaned down so that his face was even with mine. "Do us all a favor, Faith. Get help from something other than the bottle and my wife."

I flinched at his harsh words, but bit back my response.

Steven led his wife away, and she tossed a hand over her shoulder. "Tootles," she crowed, then fell into Steven, laughing.

Almost instantly, Luke slid into the seat Penelope had vacated. "How about I take you home?" he said.

I scoffed. And I tried like hell to suppress how much Steven's words stung. "You just want to sleep with me."

"I'm not denying that I would like to share your bed again, but taking advantage of a woman who's been drinking all night doesn't have much appeal."

We sat there staring at each other. I concentrated on not sounding as drunk as Penelope had. "What angle is Marla Manfield fishing for?"

"Who?"

"The pretty television reporter from Lexington."

"Oh, her. Was she pretty? I hadn't noticed."

I narrowed my gaze, and he realized I wasn't joking around.

"She thinks I'm here to find out more about Ethan."

Proving I wasn't crazy for suggesting the same thing. "Aren't you?"

"I'm here to do a job, Faith. If Ethan is mixed up in this, I will figure that out. I follow the evidence. The chief and I invited you to help with the case. You've refused so far. Is this you changing your mind?"

"I'm not an investigator. All I know how to do is operate a camera."

"So you've said. But I think you can help stop these murders." He slid from the booth and held out a hand. "Come on. I'll take you home."

I refused his hand but climbed out of the booth. When I passed by him, he placed a hand at the small of my back. Then he leaned in and whispered, a smile in his tone, "You can act like you don't enjoy having me around, but I know better."

NINETEEN

Garrett Jansen asked me to Junior Prom. I was seventeen, had never dated anyone seriously, and had had a crush on Garrett since I was a freshman—so of course I said yes. Whereas I was the quiet, academic type, Garrett was a popular athlete, like Ethan. Both were on the baseball team, and both were expected to represent Paynes Creek High School with athletic scholarships at Division I colleges after graduation.

But that meant Ethan and Garret knew each other, and after quickly asking my best friend, Amy, to go to prom with him, Ethan then persuaded Garrett to make it a double date, saying he would spring for a limo to drive the four of us to dinner and then to the dance.

Mom and Eli were more than okay with the plan. Ethan and I could look out for each other, and no one would be tempted to drink and drive, or do anything else stupid that kids did on prom night. But I was furious with Ethan. I wanted to be alone with Garrett. This was a big deal for me, the first time in high school that anyone I actually liked had ever asked me out.

I wore a red strapless dress that night. My dark hair was swept to the side with a sparkly clip holding it in place. Mom gave me a simple diamond necklace to wear; my father had given it to her on their first anniversary. Looking back on it now, I was ridiculously made-up that night, but at the time I felt prettier than I'd ever felt in my life.

I heard him gasp behind me. I lifted my head and spotted Ethan in my bedroom mirror. He was standing in the doorway.

"You look beautiful."

I tensed, and I wasn't sure how to respond. So I smiled and responded the way a sister should. "You look rather dapper yourself." He was wearing a traditional black tuxedo with a purple bow tie and matching pocket hand-kerchief—probably chosen to match Amy's dress. I approached him. "Here, let me straighten your tie." He had rented a real bow tie; no clip-on for Ethan. "There." I patted his chest. "Amy will have the most handsome date at prom."

He grabbed my hand, prompting me to meet his hard stare. "Be careful tonight," he said.

I narrowed my gaze. "Of course. But aren't we still going together?" Why had he gotten so serious?

"Yes, but I can't possibly be around you the entire night. If Garrett tries anything, I'll cut off his pitching hand."

I cocked my head, studying his expression. When he smiled, I relaxed. "Don't be silly. We're going to have so much fun."

He started to say something further, but the doorbell rang.

My eyes widened with excitement. "That should be Garrett." I grabbed his hand. "Let's go."

Our prom theme was "A Night at the Oscars." The gym had been transformed into a beautiful ballroom fit for Hollywood glamour. The entrance even had a long red carpet where a photographer took everyone's pictures.

Since Ethan, Amy, Garrett, and I arrived together, we got a picture of the four of us, with Ethan and me standing in the middle. As Ethan stood beside me with his arm around Amy, he also slipped an arm around my back, clinching my waist and rubbing his thumb against my ribcage.

As soon as the photographer snapped the picture, Ethan leaned into me and whispered, "Remember what I said," just before Garrett whisked me off in the direction of some friends.

Garrett and I had fun that night, dancing and hanging out with his friends. And when the night was over, I was sure Garrett would kiss me and ask me out again.

He didn't.

The limo driver drove Garrett home first, then Amy. Ethan walked Amy to her door, ever the gentleman. He did not kiss her goodnight. Instead they hugged, and Amy waved at me again. They'd never been more than friends.

When Ethan climbed back in the car, he declared, "Well, that was fun. But you know that Garrett isn't right for you, right?"

I stared at him. "What are you talking about? We were prom dates, not getting engaged to be married."

"You could have fooled me. And him. You were hanging on him like a girl desperate for a boyfriend."

"What?" I snapped. "You're an asshole. And you've been drinking."

"Well, so was Garrett. You know what he was saying about you in the bathroom tonight?"

I shook my head at Ethan in disbelief and turned toward the window.

"He told everyone that he couldn't believe his luck. That he had planned on having his way with you after prom until your brother ruined his night by tagging along as your chaperone."

"He did not," I said. "You're making that up just to make me not like him."

"Faith…" Ethan said. He reached across the seat and scooped up my hand. "When are you going to understand? None of the losers at our school is worthy of you."

I turned to face him. "I just wanted to have some fun, Ethan."

"Didn't you? Have fun, that is?"

"Yes, but…" I looked out the window again.

"But what?" He squeezed my hand. "Tell me. You used to tell me everything."

"I wanted him to kiss me."

Ethan's face hardened, but he quickly recovered. "I'm not going to pretend that I'm sorry he didn't. You deserve better than Garrett Jansen."

"What's wrong with Garrett?"

"He's a typical jock. He's not nice to girls. Have you ever seen him be friends with the girls he's dated?"

I thought about it. "I've never thought about it."

"Well, I've watched him. The girls he's 'dated' hate him after it's over. Just ask Martha Halloway. She made out with him two weekends in a row. When she demanded that he take her on a real date, they agreed to go to the movies. He stood her up."

"Really?"

"Yep, and when she got to school on Monday, he was

hanging all over Martha's best friend. He'd hooked up with her over the weekend."

"How have I not heard about this?"

"Because you never go to these parties. You're always studying."

"That's not true. You and I hang out plenty."

"And I will never treat you the way Garrett treats girls."

"Of course you won't," I said. "But you *have* to treat me well. You're my brother, which means you have to love me unconditionally."

When the limo dropped us off at home, it was almost two a.m., and Mom was asleep on the sofa. Ethan put a blanket over her.

"That's so cute that she tried to wait up for us," I said.

"You hungry?" he asked me.

"I would love some ice cream."

"I think I saw Blue Bell Cookie Dough in there earlier."

"You're on."

Ethan and I shared a huge bowl of ice cream while I talked about all the girls' dresses, and we gossiped about prom couples we were most surprised about.

"Did you see Tabitha?" Ethan asked.

"Yes! I was shocked when Travis walked in with her."

"Why? She's always going to parties in Paynes Creek in the summers. She obviously still knows people over here."

"Yeah, but she transferred to a school in Lexington like three years ago." I shrugged, then dipped my spoon for another bite of ice cream. "I thought she looked fat."

He smiled. And then I laughed and nearly snorted ice cream out my nose. Tabitha looked like a supermodel, and everyone at prom noticed.

"You always did hate her."

"Hate's a strong word," I said.

Ethan walked over to the radio Mom kept in the kitchen and turned it to some soft music. "I never got to dance with you tonight." He held out a hand.

Part of me thought I should refuse, but another part wanted to finish the night with him. So we danced there in the middle of our farmhouse kitchen. Two best friends—siblings—thrown together by marriage.

When the song ended, Ethan touched a finger to my chin and lifted my face so that our eyes could meet. The look in his eye was one I had seen many times. He leaned in and kissed me softly on the lips, then hugged me to him.

Seconds later, I heard footsteps behind me, so I backed away from Ethan just as Mom entered the kitchen. "Did you two have fun? I didn't even hear you come in."

"We did," Ethan said, his voice upbeat.

My mind raced as I searched for something to say, but I came up empty.

"And you're having ice cream without me?" Mom said. "I bet you already talked about everybody's dresses."

"Not you, too," Ethan said with a dramatic roll of the eyes. "Well—Faith was the belle of the ball. Of course." He winked at me. "And I'm sure she'll give you the rundown on everyone else."

"Faith, honey, did you have fun? Was Garrett a gentleman?"

I cleared my throat, barely recovered from the moment Ethan and I had just shared. "Yeah, he was, Mom. We had a great time. But I'm kind of tired. Can I tell you everything tomorrow?"

"Sure, honey." She tried, and failed, to not look disappointed.

I gave her a hug and, with a quick glance at Ethan, said, "Good night."

Ethan smiled. "Good night, Faith."

Ethan didn't mention the kiss the next day. Just like the kissing on my sixteenth birthday, we kept it private, never talking about it, not even to each other.

And when neither of us ended up going out with our dates again after prom, Mom cut our dates out of the photo we'd had taken that night. She framed the picture of Ethan and me and set it on the living room mantel, where it stayed.

TWENTY

Media swarmed the front of the police station the next morning. Despite the overcast weather, I wore oversized sunglasses—my head was about to explode from too much bourbon the night before—but they didn't prevent Marla from recognizing me as I approached.

She tapped her cameraman's arm, and he immediately turned his camera on me. Marla took several quick steps in my direction. Not even three-inch heels slowed her down.

"Miss Day," she said in her news-reporting voice. "Can you tell us why the FBI is looking into the deaths of Eli Gentry and your mother, Scarlett Day? Did you know they were reopening the case?"

I stopped and faced her, irritated at how the motion caused even more pain in the area behind my right eye. "Just in case you are not aware, I don't work for the FBI. I have no idea whether or not they are looking into that decade-old case, Marla. Move on."

Other reporters began to show interest and walk toward me.

"Are you aware that the FBI has found a link between

the recent arson cases and the fire that killed your mother and stepfather? How have you come to grips with the fact that your brother was wrongly incarcerated after your mother's death?"

I shoved past Marla and the other reporters firing questions at me, and I didn't slow until I was through the double doors.

I thought back to the three missed calls from Luke that I'd found on my phone when I awoke. I hadn't bothered to call him back, but now I wondered if I should have. Had he wanted to warn me about this?

"They're vultures, aren't they?" Penelope said. Her hair was curled to perfection, and she was wearing a bright orange and hot pink sweater set and a colorful jeweled necklace.

I lifted my glasses and squinted at her bright, cheery face. "Why do you look like *that* and I look like *this*?" I gestured to my gray down jacket, black crew-neck sweater underneath, blue jeans, and black boots. My long, straight hair was pulled into a simple ponytail that hung down my back like the short mane of a thoroughbred racehorse.

"Must be the green smoothie I had this morning. Want me to make you one?"

"No, I don't." I turned and looked out the front doors. "Marla was speaking some nonsense about the FBI reopening my mother's case."

Penelope didn't say anything.

I rotated my head slowly in her direction. "Tell me Marla has no idea what she's talking about."

Penelope looked down at her shoes—rose-colored suede flats—then back at me. She let out a sigh. "Oh, honey, I'm sorry. I thought someone would have told you."

Yelling sounded from the chief's office. Through the open blinds of the window that separated the chief from his station house, I saw Uncle Henry lean across the chief's desk, lift a hand, and point it in Chief Reid's face. "You told me they weren't digging up old skeletons!"

"Henry, I need you to calm down," Chief Reid said. He leaned away from Uncle Henry's wagging finger. He appeared calm but spoke in a loud voice. "I wasn't given much of a choice. And it didn't help that Ethan was released."

A sweat broke out across the back of my neck. Without taking my eyes off of the two men, I asked Penelope, "Where's Special Agent Justice?"

"I'm told he gathered up several boxes of evidence and relocated."

I swiveled my head toward Penelope. "Relocated? What does that mean? He left town?" It pissed me off that this stirred up emotions inside me.

She shrugged. "I don't think so. He's staying out your way, at Cooper Adams's place. Coop remodeled the barn, turned it into an apartment. In case you didn't already know. I think that's where Luke is living while he's here." There was a mischievous look in her eye, but she refrained from voicing the question I knew was on her mind.

Uncle Henry's raised voice made itself heard once more. "If this turns out badly, Sam, I'm holding you personally responsible!" Then he spun around and jerked open the chief's office door.

Immediately, he spotted me across the room—and froze. Everyone in the station turned and stared at me, and I was sure they could all feel the tension that hung between Uncle Henry and me.

"Faith," he said.

As much as I wanted to discuss this latest development with both him and Chief Reid, I wanted to hear Luke's version even more. So I spun on my heel, opened the doors, and darted right back out into the vultures.

———————

THE SKIES BEGAN SPITTING a mixture of sleet and freezing rain as I drove the country roads toward Cooper's place. At first I barreled through it, but when my tires slid on a patch of ice—luckily I recovered quickly—I decided to slow way down. A good idea, as the storm only grew in intensity from there.

At Coop's, I pulled up next to the barn, shrugged into my coat, gloves, and winter toboggan, and stepped out of the car. Pellets of ice smacked against my face.

I knew this area well. For many years, Mr. Kuster hosted Fourth of July parties here, complete with hayrides and bonfires, and winter sleigh-riding parties, which also included bonfires, but with the added warmth of hot chocolate. Mom took Finch and me to those parties when we were young, and later—after Finch was gone—Ethan and I continued the tradition on our own. But now the area looked empty—no cars or trucks, no sign that anyone was here.

I approached the normal-sized door to the right of the large barn doors. I knocked on it and listened.

Nothing.

I knocked again, then yelled out. "Luke! Coop!"

I tried the doorknob; it was unlocked. I shouldn't just walk in, though. A reasonable person would call Luke on his cell phone, not trespass into his residence. But then again, it was a barn—it didn't feel like stepping into someone's house. And technically I was already trespassing, and had been from the minute I drove onto the property.

Inside, I yelled again. "Luke? Coop? Anyone home?"

This part of the barn was still a barn, complete with rafters above, several stalls for horses—though I saw no animals—farm equipment, and the familiar tractor that pulled the trailer during hayrides. But on the opposite side of the barn, new wood had been put up to section off a smaller area. This must be the renovated apartment Penelope had mentioned.

I knocked on the door to the apartment and still got no response. Once again I let myself in.

Coop had done an amazing job. I stepped into a charming, rustic living room decorated with a masculine but comfortable decor in plaids, soft browns, and grays, with occasional splashes of red and black. All the fabrics chosen with the hopes that they would hide dirt, most likely. If I had to guess, Coop had not done all this decorating alone.

To one side was a kitchenette with a microwave and coffee pot, but no oven. Enough for a bachelor to survive on, though not nearly enough to fill up the farm table, which seated six. I touched the coffee pot—still warm.

A spiral staircase led upward. I walked over and called up the dark wooden stairs. "Luke!"

He clearly wasn't here, and at this point I was just being nosy. But I'd come this far…

I climbed the stairs to a loft bedroom that housed an unmade king-sized bed, two bedside tables, and a couple of chairs. Black-framed windows stretched along the outside wall, overlooking the woods that separated Coop's land from mine. On the other side of the room was another distressed farm table, covered in paper and books, clearly being used as a desk. An equally distressed wrought-iron chandelier hung above it, and had been left on. Between the light being left on and the warm coffee pot, I knew Luke hadn't been gone long, and might return soon. I should go.

I started to head back down the spiral steps, but I couldn't when I noticed what was hanging on the wall on the other side of the table.

An evidence board.

It hung on the wall behind the table, stretching its length. More than a dozen photos hung in a zigzag pattern. Twine stretched from photos to newspaper articles to Post-It notes. I stepped closer, and my attention was immediately drawn to two photos placed side by side near the top of the board, just to the left of the center.

Both were pictures of me.

One was from when I was seventeen; the other was from just last year, my official identification photo taken when I became an associate of the Paynes Creek PD.

Just to the left of my photos was a mug shot of Ethan taken after his arrest. Twine stretched from our pictures to a newspaper article about Ethan's trial. The headline read: *Stepsister Testifies Against Stepbrother in Paynes Creek Murder Case.* An artist's sketch showed me with one hand on the Bible and the other held in the air, obviously swearing to tell the truth, the whole truth, and nothing but the truth.

Nearby I spotted photos of Uncle Henry, Aunt Leah, and even Finch.

Why were these photos on Luke's evidence board? Ethan's photo... that much I understood. But me? And so recent? What exactly was Luke investigating, anyway?

TWENTY-ONE

"What are you doing here?"

At the sound of Luke's voice, I spun around and sucked in an audible gasp. "I... I was looking for you."

"Then maybe try answering your phone. I called you three times this morning, and I just got back from driving over to your place. The roads are getting bad out there."

"The roads are getting bad?" I repeated. "That's what you want to say to me?"

"I didn't know—"

"You didn't know what, Luke? That you were going to include me on your wall of arson and murder suspects when you slept with me?"

"No. I didn't know they were going to announce the reopening of your mother's murder case this morning."

"But you *did* know they were reopening it? Yet you said nothing about it last night." I started across the room. "I have to go. This was a mistake."

Luke stretched an arm across my chest to block me from passing. His fingers wrapped around my upper arm.

I jerked backwards. "Don't touch me." Heat spread up

my spine and onto my cheeks. I broke out into a cold sweat.

Luke let go of me, but stepped in front of me to keep me from leaving. "Give me ten minutes to explain."

I let my eyes lift to meet his determined gaze. There was a mixture of confidence, concern, and fear in his eyes, shadowed by furrowed brows.

"You don't deserve the opportunity to explain," I said. "And I will not risk incriminating myself in your hunt for a serial killer." Tears stung my eyes at the realization that I had slept with a man who thought I was capable of such horrific crimes. "Let me pass, Luke, or you'll be hauling me to the police station for assaulting you."

"Faith…"

My face hardened further.

He stepped aside, and I rushed past him.

"At least let me give you a ride," he said from behind me. "The roads have gotten slick, and you're upset."

I didn't acknowledge his concern. And I didn't stop until I was outside, behind the steering wheel, and away from Luke Justice.

Aunt Leah made me a mug of tea—chamomile, to relax me. I wanted bourbon, but she hated how much I drank.

"Now tell me what's got you so worked up," she said as she set the steaming mug and a container of fresh local honey in front of me.

I grabbed the plastic bear bottle and squeezed a stream of honey into the tea. "What if everyone was wrong about Ethan, Aunt Leah? What if he didn't do it?"

"Faith—what are you talking about? Ethan deserved

his sentence. And to be honest, I'm truly sorry they let him out."

"But how can you be so convinced? He loved his father, and Mom was more of a mother to him than his own mother had ever been."

"The investigation was thorough. The empty gas cans were discovered in his car. He would have disposed of them had he not stopped to pull you out of the fire. And thank God for that. That was the only thing he did that kept me from wishing for the death penalty."

"But... empty gas cans? That's it? There were no fingerprints on those gas cans. And they didn't find gloves at the scene." I sounded like a better defense attorney than the one Ethan had at his trial.

"Faith, what's gotten into you? You know all the facts as well as I do. You know he killed your mom."

The front door slammed, and Uncle Henry appeared at the door to the kitchen. "I guess you've both heard," he said as a greeting.

"I heard you arguing with Chief Reid," I said, turning back around in my seat. I lifted the tea to my lips and blew on it before taking a sip.

"I've got a call in to my contact at the Bureau," Uncle Henry said. "I plan to send that sorry-ass excuse for an FBI agent packing as quickly as possible."

He was clearly beyond angry. His face was red as if overheated, and he seemed to be breathing heavier than usual.

It had been a long time since I'd heard Uncle Henry swear.

Did I tell my aunt and uncle that the "sorry-ass excuse for an FBI agent" had me at the top of his evidence board?

"Now, Henry," Aunt Leah said, placing a hand on his

cheek as if she were taking his temperature. "Don't go giving yourself a heart attack."

The front door slammed again, and two seconds later, Finch entered the kitchen. "Want to tell me how the FBI got the authority to reopen Mom's case? This wasn't a federal investigation. Why would it be considered one now?"

"I'm working on it," Uncle Henry said. "What are you doing here?"

"Took a long lunch. Aubrey was having some chest pain and a little difficulty breathing when I checked on her earlier."

"What?" Aunt Leah said.

"It's okay, I got her to the doctor, and he said she was just having a panic attack. She says she got herself worked up over something she read in one of those parenting books, but if you ask me, this case being reopened is what stressed her out. Anyway," he waved a hand, "she's under strict orders to stay in bed for a few days and relax."

"It sounds serious," I said. "Want me to go over there?"

"I'm sure she'd love to see you. She's sleeping now, but maybe later."

"Well, sit down," Aunt Leah said. "I'll whip us all up some soup and sandwiches. And I'll send some home with you for Aubrey."

Uncle Henry leaned in and kissed his wife on the cheek. "I'm going to go make a phone call. Call me when lunch is ready."

Finch pulled out a chair and sat across from me. "So, is this your friend's doing?"

"My friend?" I asked.

"Word on the street is you've gotten all chummy with that fed."

"Chummy?"

"Aunt Leah, is there an echo in here?"

Aunt Leah waved a hand. "I just think Faith is stalling because she doesn't like the tone of your interrogation. And honestly, neither do I."

"Let me put it another way," Finch said. "What's going on with you and Special Agent Justice?"

"Nothing. I've just been photographing the crime scenes—in other words, my job." I didn't dare mention that my photograph was up on Luke's evidence wall—and I certainly wasn't going to tell him that *his* picture was there, too. That would get him worked up over nothing; he wasn't even in Paynes Creek the night of the fire.

"Have you seen Ethan again?" Finch asked.

Aunt Leah spun around, shock and worry on her face. "You saw Ethan? When?"

I narrowed my eyes at Finch. "Thanks a lot."

He shrugged. "I assumed you'd told them."

Aunt Leah stopped what she was doing and faced me. "When and where did you see Ethan? Is that why you came over? Did he hurt you?"

"No. I happened into the Spotted Cat. Apparently he's working there." I left out the part about last night's little visit.

"You just *happened* into a Lexington dive bar where Ethan just *happened* to work?" Finch said.

Uncle Henry walked back into the kitchen. "He's not just working there," he said. "He owns it."

"Owns it?" I said. "How did he manage to buy a bar? He just got out of prison three weeks ago."

Uncle Henry shrugged. "He used his inheritance."

"What inheritance?" I asked.

Finch gave him a hard look. "Uncle Henry, you didn't."

"Someone please explain what the hell is going on here."

Uncle Henry walked to the refrigerator and grabbed a soda. "I received a call from our bank president two weeks ago. He told me that Ethan had come in wanting to use his share of your parents' land as collateral to purchase a piece of property."

I couldn't believe it. "He wanted to use the land *I* live on as collateral for a loan, and you didn't think to *tell* me?"

"I'm telling you now. Ethan needed the money and he still has a right to one third of that land. I spoke to an attorney. He suggested that if the two of you didn't want to be forced to sell the land, that you would need to buy Ethan out."

Crap. "I don't have that kind of money," I said. "I guess I could get a loan. Take money out of my retirement."

Uncle Henry lifted a gentle hand. "I bought out Ethan."

"Oh, Uncle Henry," Finch said. "I'll pay you back. And we can—"

"No. It's been done. My attorney is drawing up the paperwork for me to gift that third of the land to the two of you, along with an agreement that Faith can live on the land for as long as she wishes."

Finch nodded. "Of course she can."

I stood and threw my arms around Uncle Henry. "I don't know what to say, except thank you."

"You don't even need to say that. You two are our family." He pulled his wife closer and put an arm around her. She smiled at both of us. "We are both so very proud of you."

While I was thankful for how that had worked out, I was curious as to why Ethan would give up ties to the land he grew up on—ties to me.

But then I remembered what he did to me, and I asked myself: Had he not gone to prison for murder, would I have been able to send him to prison for assaulting me?

"I'm not feeling well," I said. "The weather is supposed to get worse. I think I better get home before I get stuck in town."

"Oh, honey. Why don't you stay here? Your room has fresh sheets. I don't want to worry about you."

I gave Aunt Leah a hug, then Uncle Henry. "I'll be fine. I'll text you when I get home."

"I'll walk you out," Finch said, getting up from the table.

When we reached the front door, Finch grabbed my shoulders and turned me to face him. "You okay with what Uncle Henry did?"

"Of course. Are you? You're entitled to request rent from me, you know."

"Don't be ridiculous." He pulled me in for a quick hug and released me.

"Tell Aubrey I'll call her later."

TWENTY-TWO

The sleet and freezing rain switched over to snow in the early afternoon. School let out early, and businesses were letting employees go home. The local weather people promised a nasty evening commute. But this was Kentucky; this type of weather never stuck around long, and it was rarely as bad as predicted.

There was one news van sitting outside the police station as I passed. The others had gone back to Lexington, or moved on to cover the road conditions. They'd be back, though. Hard to keep pesky flies off cow patties.

When I turned the corner past the police station, I spotted two teenage girls headed toward the park: Bella Reynolds and Alexandra Sims. Sadly, Sadie Porter was missing from the Three Musketeers, as they were known. On a whim, I decided to see what I could learn from them.

I circled around and parked in the lot between the library and the park, close to where Ethan and I used to park after school. Thankfully, I had boots in my vehicle; photographing crime scenes, especially fires, could be hell on a nice pair of shoes. I slipped them on, got out, and walked into the park.

The girls were sitting on the swings, facing away from me. Alexandra pulled something from her pocket, put a lighter to one end, and took a drag. A joint? No—a bong.

Putting my phone to my ear and acting like I was involved in conversation, I walked around into their field of view, though not too close. I knew the moment they spotted me. Bella was taking a hit when Alexandra motioned for her to stop.

"Put it away," I heard her whisper.

I had an idea on how to get closer.

"I don't care, asshole!" I screamed into the phone. "We are through. Finished. Get your shit and get out of my house… No, I won't give you another chance." I walked toward the girls, still pretending not to notice them. "And if you don't leave the money you owe me on the kitchen table, I'm sending my attorney after you… Go ahead, call the chief. I don't work for the Paynes Creek PD. I'm my own boss."

I was no more than ten yards from them when I looked down at my phone. "That piece of shit hung up on me," I muttered, talking to myself. I lifted my head, and recoiled slightly when I saw Bella and Alexandra swinging. "Oh. Sorry. I was so caught up in my own bullshit, I didn't even see you two."

I turned and started to walk away. I would have to come up with a Plan B if this didn't work, but I was hoping—

"You look like you could use a hit," Bella called.

"Bella…" Alexandra warned.

"Oh, I think she's cool with it. Aren't you, Faith?" Bella held out the bong.

"Is that a flute?" I asked. I was impressed that they'd crafted a bong from a musical instrument.

"Yeah." Bella shrugged. "I also made one out of pieces of a trumpet. My mom thought they were projects for my art class. But that one was destroyed in the fire."

I took the makeshift bong and a lighter from her. "Very clever." I lifted the bong to my mouth and took a hit.

Bella pulled a bottle from her bag. "Peppermint schnapps," she said when I lifted a brow. "I thought it appropriate on the first real snow day. It's going to go well with a hot chocolate when I get home, but for now..." She shrugged, unscrewed the top, and took a large drink.

If I got caught smoking marijuana and drinking alcohol with a couple of high school kids, a reopened murder investigation would be the least of my worries. I handed the flute-bong back to Bella. "Sorry about your parents." I looked to Alexandra, who was now taking a gulp of the schnapps. "And your friend."

"Thanks," Alexandra said. "Do they know who's setting these fires?"

I looked up toward the police station. "No, unfortunately. But I know they're doing everything they can to find out."

"You know what we're going through, don't you?" Bella said. For a girl who'd just lost both of her parents and one of her best friends, she didn't sound as sad as I would have expected. Maybe she was hiding her sorrow in alcohol and drugs. I did that for a time. It didn't work.

"I think everyone handles grief and loss differently," I said. "But I know what I went through. It sucked." Those were the most honest two words I could have said.

Both girls nodded.

Bella laughed and nudged her friend. "But this weed sure is some good shit, right?"

Alexandra flashed her a look somewhere between despair and confusion, but then her lips slid into an easy grin. "Yeah." She followed it with a giggle. The effects of the pot and alcohol were taking over. By the looks of the half-empty bottle, this wasn't their first drink of the day.

"This *is* some good stuff," I agreed. "Where did you get it?"

Both girls stiffened. Had I not been watching for it, I would have missed it.

"I'm asking for a friend." I smiled, hoping they would think I wanted my own supply sometime. Even though I'd given up marijuana long ago.

"Just a kid from school," Bella said.

"Yeah," Alexandra scoffed. "A *big* kid." She rolled her eyes.

Bella shot Alexandra a hard stare.

"What?" Alexandra said. "We don't owe him anything. It's not like Matt delivered on any of *his* promises yet."

Matt? As in Matthew Lake? "Are you telling me Mr. Lake scored you this weed?" I shook my head. "Man, times sure have changed. What I would have given to have had cool teachers like Mr. Lake."

"Yeah, he's cool," Bella said. She was studying me, wondering if she could trust me. I could almost see her body go from head-to-toe tension to muscle-by-muscle relaxation. "Did you screw your stepbrother?" she blurted out.

"Bella!" Alexandra said.

I took the bong from Bella and took another hit. It really was some good marijuana. "Did you screw your teacher?" I fired back.

A smile spread across Bella's face. "Yes, and there's nothing anyone can do about it. I'm eighteen as of yesterday, and he's no longer a teacher. He's getting me an audition at Juilliard. Alexandra, too."

I raised both brows. "Really? Has either of these auditions been scheduled?"

"Not yet, but he went there, and he knows people in admissions."

"Congratulations," I said, but I no more believed that Matthew Lake would get Bella and Alexandra an audition at Juilliard than I believed my stepbrother's recent transaction with Henry meant he was planning to disappear from my life. Nothing was that easy.

"So, did you?" Bella asked. "Did you have sex with Ethan Gentry before he went all psycho?"

When I didn't answer, Alexandra stopped swinging. "You did, didn't you?" She slid a sly glance toward her friend, letting her know she was sorry she had doubted her.

"It's not like they're related," Bella said. "I don't see anything wrong with it."

"Well *I* do," Alexandra said. "It's practically incest."

"It is not." Bella laughed while kicking her feet out and swinging higher.

"If you think sex between two step-siblings is inappropriate," I said to Alexandra, "then what do you think of sex between a minor and a person of authority?"

They both giggled, clearly buzzed. "I never had sex with Matthew," Alexandra answered.

Bella laughed. "No, but you *did* send him the photos he wanted…"

Now we were getting somewhere. Bella and Alexandra were in deep with this Matthew Lake, who was obviously the predator the town thought he was. It was sad, when I thought about it, that no one seemed to be protecting these girls.

Alexandra shrugged. "A girl's gotta do what a girl's

gotta do to get out of a shithole town like Paynes Creek."

"Bella," I said, "I know this has been hard on you, but I'm curious about something… How long did your parents know about your relationship with Mr. Lake before they reported it?"

She slowed her swinging. "You know… I loved my parents, but they were so hypocritical. They knew Matthew and I were growing closer. They didn't have a problem until Matthew and I had our first fight."

"What was the fight about?" I asked.

"I was pissed off because I found photos of Sadie and Alexandra on his phone."

Alexandra seemed to shrink a little.

"And then," Bella continued, "when I confronted Sadie, she got pissed off and crazy jealous and told her parents about Matthew and me."

"When was this?"

"When did Sadie tell her parents Matthew and I were a couple?"

I nodded.

"Oh, months ago."

"Did Sadie's parents say anything to your parents? I mean, I know your parents knew something was going on, but did Sadie's parents get involved?"

"Nope."

"They didn't care," Alexandra said with a shrug. "They also knew that Matthew had pictures of me. But they never said anything to my parents."

"Do your parents know now?" I asked, shocked at what these two kids were telling me.

"God, no! My parents would have me in a convent and Mr. Lake in jail if they ever found out," Alexandra said. "That is, if my dad didn't shove a shotgun up his ass first." She chuckled as if imagining her father doing just that.

"Sadie's parents knew that Juilliard would never award more than one scholarship to someone from Paynes Creek High School, and they thought Sadie was more talented than me. I think they didn't want to get Matthew in trouble until Sadie got an audition with Juilliard."

"You're telling me that Sadie's parents knew that Matthew was collecting photos of their daughter and that he was engaging in a relationship with a student, but they said nothing out of fear that their daughter wouldn't get her shot at Juilliard?"

Alexandra nodded. "When you put it like that, it sounds really messed up." She turned to her friend. "I loved Sadie, but she wasn't as talented as you. You still would have gotten the scholarship over her."

"Aww, thanks." Bella swung over and leaned into her friend. "I loved her, too."

"She was such a head case," Alexandra said, kicking her legs back and forth in the swing. "I hope they find who's doing this. And leave Matthew alone. He would never hurt a fly. He's really a kind person."

I wasn't sure how kind Matthew Lake was, but I also wasn't quick to consider him a serious suspect for murder. Still, I planned to turn over this information to Luke.

I turned to leave. "Well, thanks for the hit. You girls better get home. You're not driving, are you?"

"No. We're just walking up to Alexandra's house, up the hill."

I was heading for my vehicle when I realized I had one more question. I turned back to them. They had already hopped off the swings. "Alexandra, when you said Sadie was a head case, what did you mean by that?"

"She'd been going to a therapist for months. Depression and anxiety. That's probably how her parents found out about her and Matt."

TWENTY-THREE

When I finally pulled into my driveway, I breathed a sigh of gratitude that I had made it home safely. The roads were terrible, and the snow was coming down even harder than the meteorologists had predicted.

My phone rang just as I shut off my engine. It was Luke. I declined his call. I was still angry with him, but I would call him back when I got inside so that I could tell him about my conversation with Bella and Alexandra.

I immediately received a text.

Please pick up. I need to tell you something.

My phone rang again. With a huff, I answered.

"What do you want? I was planning to call you."

"Ethan wasn't working any of the nights that someone broke into your trailer or started those bonfires on your property. Meaning, he doesn't have an alibi for the murders or the nights your home was broken into."

"Okay. That's unfortunate for him, but that doesn't mean—"

"And you said he went to your place the other night before you came to Boone's."

"Yeah. So? All coincidences. Surely even you, big shot FBI agent, know that these things don't make him guilty of anything." But I closed my eyes and squeezed the bridge of my nose. Despite my protests, I was terrified that Luke was right.

"He's stalking you, Faith. He ditched his tails the other night before showing up there. I don't think you should be alone until we figure out what's going on."

"Oh, and I suppose you're going to suggest that you come over and protect me?"

"Actually, I was hoping to put a uniform at the end of your driveway, and another directly in front of your trailer."

"Yeah? Are you also going to put one in *your* driveway and block the path between Coop's barn and here?"

"What do you mean by that?"

"Whoever was on my property the night of the second bonfire had to have run through the woods to get away. I'm guessing they parked at or near Coop's."

"Dammit. There're too many access points."

"Listen, I can take care of myself. But if it makes you feel better to put someone at the end of my driveway, I won't fight it."

"Great. Now... I wish you'd let me explain my evidence wall. I never suspected you in any of the crimes. But I do think you could fill in some holes."

"Then why didn't you just ask?"

"I was warming up to it."

"By sleeping with me?"

"That wasn't part of the plan. It just happened because you're so damn sexy."

I had a tough time believing that Luke found me the least bit sexy after seeing me naked. I'd seen my scars. They'd followed me like a dark storm cloud my whole life.

Men had turned away from me more times than I could count. And most of them hadn't gotten as close as Luke did. He would be no different.

"Look," he said, "let me come over. We can talk through my evidence. You can shed some light on some of my unanswered questions. Maybe you can help me move someone to the top of the suspect list. Because right now, not much makes sense."

"Fine. And I should probably tell you about my conversation with Bella Reynolds and Alexandra Sims." I quickly filled him in.

"I'm coming over. We'll talk more when I get there."

I shut off my engine and released a sigh. "Be careful. The roads are terrible."

"That's okay. I was thinking about walking through the woods. You've got me curious about the path between Coop's and there."

I pushed my way out of the vehicle into two inches of fluffy white snow. There was still a quarter inch of ice underneath, so I stepped carefully, keeping my body weight evenly dispersed. When I was almost to my trailer, I heard a sound behind me. I started to turn, but something struck me hard against the back of my head, and everything went black.

I STRUGGLED to open my eyes. I saw flashes of white amid the darkness. I was being dragged.

My jeans were sticking to my legs, cold as ice.

It was snow. I was being dragged across snow. Someone had their arms threaded through mine; my back was against their body. They were struggling with my weight.

They said nothing. I tried to turn toward my assailant,

but the moment my head began to rotate, I lost consciousness again.

MY EYES FLUTTERED OPEN, then closed. My head bobbed, my chin hitting my chest. Orange light flashed behind my lids, but I couldn't keep them open.

"Faith," a voice said. "Can you hear me?"

Heat warmed my cheeks, but I shivered. My pants were wet, and everything below my waist felt numb. The memory of being dragged through the snow flashed into my mind.

I realized I was sitting in one of the Adirondack chairs around my fire pit.

"Faith," the voice said again. A warm hand touched my face.

"Ethan?" I winced at the stinging pain in the back of my head. I touched the spot that ached. My hand came away cold and wet.

I opened my eyes, slowly. My fingers were red. Ethan's dark figure was kneeling in front of me, flames flickering behind him. I was definitely at my fire pit.

"We need to get you to the hospital. Can you walk? Or do you want me to carry you?"

"Someone hit me." I was so confused. Ethan's face went in and out of focus. "Was it you?" Panic began to form inside my chest. I lifted my hand and tried to massage a spot there. I wanted to fight Ethan, keep him from hurting me—and at the same time, I didn't want to believe he would harm me, which was stupid given our past and what Luke had told me.

"Faith, listen to me. I would never hurt you. I didn't start this fire. I drove up and saw someone throwing wood onto the pile. I don't know." He gave his head a shake as if he was trying to remember exactly what he saw. "But——"

"You did this." Tears stung my eyes. "You weren't at the bar the nights the fires were built. You were here last night. And now." My voice sounded hysterical, even to my own ears.

"I came back because of what you said last night. I'm going to prove to you that I'm not the one stalking you. But right now, we need to get you to the hospital."

"What the fuck?" Luke's voice rang out from the other side of the fire.

Ethan stood and backed away. "Who the hell are you?"

Luke drew his gun and pointed it at Ethan. "Move away from her."

"Okay." He slowly raised his hands in front of him. "The gun isn't necessary." He took a step away.

"What did you do to her?" Luke's eyes darted from Ethan to me, then back to Ethan. "Faith, talk to me. Are you okay?"

"I didn't do anything," Ethan said. "But she needs a doctor. Someone knocked her pretty good. I found her unconscious."

"I don't need a doctor," I moaned.

"Did he do this to you?" Luke asked. He walked closer and looked at the back of my head. "Faith, you're bleeding."

"I know I'm bleeding." I didn't hide my irritation. "I'm also freezing. Could someone please get me inside?"

Luke kept his gun pointed at Ethan. "Get down on the ground." He pulled his phone from his pocket, dialed a number, then brought it to his ear.

"And what are you going to do? You have handcuffs on you?" Ethan went down on his knees. "This is ridiculous. I didn't hit her. I drove up as someone was lighting that fire.

As I got closer to the fire, I realized she was unconscious, but it was too late—whoever it was took off running through the woods."

"How long ago? I didn't see anyone come through on the other side."

"I don't know. Five minutes?"

Luke turned his attention back to the phone. "This is Special Agent Luke Justice. I need an ambulance and a squad car." He rattled off the address, gave dispatch more information, and hung up.

Bracing myself on the side of the chair, I stood. "I'm so cold. I'm going inside." I took a step and swayed. The world spun around me.

Ethan sprang to his feet fast as a cat and reached out a hand. I had no choice but to grab it and steady myself.

Luke stepped forward as well, his gun still trained on Ethan.

"Don't get twitchy, man," Ethan said. "I'm only trying to help her. I swear I didn't do this to her."

"You're going to help her to the trailer," Luke replied coldly. "You try anything, and I *will* shoot you."

Ethan slid an arm around me. "I've got you."

He led me forward. Luke stayed two paces behind us, gun in hand.

As we walked, the snow and ice crunching beneath our feet, I spotted a few drops of blood in the snow, not yet completely covered up by fresher snow. I also noted two sets of footprints. One set was pointed toward my trailer, the prints wide apart, spaced around a line of flattened snow, where something was dragged. I realized that something was me.

To the left was another set of prints. They were headed in the direction of the fire pit. I looked down and examined Ethan's boots as he helped me along. He wore a pair of thick rubber snow boots with waterproof leather and wool lining covering his jeans. He was definitely prepared for the weather. His boots matched the set of prints walking toward the fire pit, but not the ones facing backwards.

The sun had set; the temperature was going down. There were at least four inches of snow on the ground already, and it didn't appear to be letting up. It looked like we were in for a night of very bad weather.

And someone had assaulted me. If it wasn't Ethan, then I was lucky he came along. If it *was* Ethan, I was lucky Luke showed up.

I supposed either way, that made me lucky.

TWENTY-FOUR

The hospital had been crazy busy with car accident victims, people who had fallen on the ice, and other weather-related accidents. When an ambulance couldn't get to us quickly enough, Luke had sent Ethan on to the station with a uniformed officer who *had* managed to get to us, and Luke drove me to the hospital.

Finch met me there so Luke could get to the station to interrogate Ethan.

It took two hours to get through triage, and after the long wait, a doctor walked in, did a quick examination, and determined that my concussion wasn't that serious and that I should go home and rest.

An hour later, armed with painkillers that were sure to make me feel dopey, Finch helped me into the police station. He had wanted to take me home to his house, but I insisted on seeing how the interrogation was going. Luke had informed me by text that they were still interviewing Ethan. It was clear to me that Ethan hadn't been the one to hit me and drag me through the snow, so I decided to make a statement so Ethan could go home.

Very few officers were milling about. My guess was a lot of them were out helping stranded drivers who'd ignored warnings to stay off the roads and were now stuck in ditches.

I walked to the viewing room; I knew Luke was interrogating Ethan, and wanted to watch. But as I entered the viewing room, I realized Finch wasn't behind me. A second later, I knew why.

Finch burst into the interview room on the other side of the window. He grabbed Ethan and shoved him up against the wall. "You never should have come back here! You ruined her life!"

"Finch! Stop!" I shouted.

I tore from the viewing room. By the time I entered the interview room, Luke and Chief Reid had pulled Finch off of Ethan.

Luke shoved Finch out into the hallway. "Go cool off. This isn't helping."

Ethan rolled his shoulders and took a couple of deep breaths. His eyes met mine, and his face softened. "Everything check out okay?" The concern in his voice squeezed my heart. No matter how hard I tried, I couldn't separate all of the events that had led us to this point. And that particular tone in his voice brought back the wonderful memories of our teen years, not the memories of the events that had ended our relationship.

But I turned and walked out of the room without a word. Luke and the chief followed.

"You ready to make a statement?" Chief asked me.

I nodded.

"Good. Because unless you have something solid, I'm not going to be able to hold him much longer. I'll be right back—gotta get the paperwork."

Luke placed a hand to my lower back and led me into

another room. When we were out of everyone's view, he placed a hand on my cheek. "What did the doctors say?"

His touch and the look in his eyes brought heat to my face. It was more intimate than I was ready for after the day I'd had, and I wasn't sure how to respond.

I backed away. "Mild concussion; killer headache."

"Are you sure you want to do this now?"

"Yes, and then I want to sleep."

Chief Reid entered with some forms, sat at the table, and began filling out my name and other information. I was surprised he even knew how to complete the paperwork himself; usually he had people to do that.

I took a seat across from him, and Luke sat next to me.

"Where'd Finch go?" I asked.

"He's in the break room on the phone," Chief said. "I've got someone watching to make sure he doesn't try to take another swing at Ethan." He looked across the table at me and sighed. "First, on behalf of the Paynes Creek PD, I want to say I'm sorry no one took your earlier complaint seriously."

I glanced at Luke, who looked like he was chomping down hard on his tongue to keep from saying anything.

"Now," Chief continued, "I know you need rest. Tell me what happened tonight so I can get you out of here."

I told Chief how I'd been in town when the roads started to get worse, and how I decided to head home. I left out the part about smoking marijuana with a pair of teenagers. "When I reached home, Luke called."

Chief turned a critical eye on Luke. I was sure he was jumping to all sorts of conclusions.

Luke explained. "I was hoping she could help me out with some aspects of my investigation. I decided I would walk through the woods to her place so that we could talk in person."

Chief made a note on the form. "Okay. Keep going."

"I hung up with Luke, got out of the car, and walked toward my trailer. I heard a sound behind me, like a footstep, and then someone clocked me. I don't remember much else. I know I was dragged through the snow. When I came to, Ethan was there, and I was sitting in a chair next to a fire in my fire pit. Ethan swore he didn't hit me or set the fire. He said he drove up and saw someone throwing wood on the fire, but that whoever it was took off into the woods."

"Do you think Ethan attacked you?"

I stared at a crumb on the table in front of me and tried to remember everything I heard and smelled and saw. But despite my perfect memory, I couldn't remember something I didn't see—and I never saw my attacker.

I looked up at the chief. "I don't think so."

Chief turned to Luke. "How long from the time you called Faith until you arrived at her farm?"

"Like I told you earlier, it had to be at least twenty minutes. I started to head right out, but I received a phone call."

"From whom?"

Luke shifted in his seat. He suddenly looked very uncomfortable. "I'll tell you that eventually if I need to, but at the moment, I'd like to keep that to myself. I don't think it has anything to do with this. If my opinion changes on that, I promise I'll reveal who it was."

Chief didn't look happy about Luke withholding information, but he turned back to me. "Can you give me any reason to lock that son of a bitch up?"

I shook my head slowly. "Actually, I can't."

"How can you be so sure?"

"Because when we were leaving the fire pit, I noticed the tracks in the snow—they were starting to be covered up, but I could still see them. One set of tracks was widely spaced around drag marks. The footprints were pointed toward my trailer—I assume because whoever was dragging me was walking backwards. The second set of prints was different—not the same shoes. So there were two people there. Either Ethan is telling the truth, and he arrived after I was attacked, or he had a partner who took off before Luke arrived."

Luke leaned back in his seat and ran a hand through his hair. "Well, hell! That matches up perfectly with Ethan's story."

WHILE I WAS at the police station, Finch was called away for a veterinary emergency. I asked him if he wanted me to go stay with Aubrey—to do my part to keep her in bed, resting—but he said I needed to take care of myself tonight.

Ethan left, too—the police had no reason to keep him, and an officer drove him back to his car, which was still at my trailer. I didn't give Ethan a chance to talk to me before he left, though I could see how he badly wanted a moment alone with me.

That left me with Luke Justice.

"Take me to your place," I said once he and I were settled in his SUV. I knew I shouldn't be alone after suffering a concussion.

His expression was serious at first, then a grin slid across his face. "Thought you'd never ask."

I rolled my eyes and leaned back against the seat, cupping my hand over my forehead. My headache remained. "I want to look at your evidence board."

"Faith…" His tone went back to serious.

"Look," I said. "I'm obviously tied to this. Immediately after all three recent arson cases, someone has set a fire in my yard and broken into my trailer. And today, someone assaulted me. Either Ethan is involved, or someone wants me to *believe* Ethan is involved. Like it or not, I'm in this deep. You said you'd ruled me out as a suspect, and you've already invited me to get involved. So I accept your invitation. I want to see your evidence."

He faced forward and started the vehicle. "Fine. But you're going to take your medicine and sleep off that headache first."

"Agreed." The pain was excruciating, and I wasn't sure I could process any new information in that state anyway.

"And you're going to tell me the whole truth about what happened the night your mom was killed."

I stared out the windshield. Luke Justice would get more than he bargained for if and when I ever started being honest about that night.

TWENTY-FIVE

I wasn't sure how much later it was when I awoke in Luke Justice's bed, alone. A single soft lamp was lit in a far corner. Luke had let me wear one of his sweatshirts—from Georgetown University, his alma mater—and I had draped my jeans across the end of the bed.

Now I pushed off the blankets, slipped on my jeans, and padded downstairs in sock feet.

I found Luke asleep on the couch. Apparently he hadn't intended to nap: he had glasses on, and a thick booklet of white computer paper was turned upside down on his chest. He'd probably just decided to "rest his eyes."

I smiled at the image before me. I'd never seen him in glasses; he probably wore contacts most of the time. He looked handsome and smart in the wire rims. And I believed that he was a kind man. It was unfortunate for him that he'd stumbled into a case involving me and my dark history.

I walked quietly to the kitchenette and got a glass of water from the tap. I was tempted to take more medicine, but I wanted to have a clear head for a while.

"How are you feeling?" Luke asked behind me. His voice sounded groggy.

I turned. "Like someone scrambled my egg."

He sat up, set the booklet and his glasses on the coffee table, and rubbed his eyes. Then he stood up and walked over to me. His fingers went immediately to my forehead and traced a line from there down to my jawline. They were cool and slightly calloused to the touch. "It's two a.m. Why don't you sleep a little more?"

"Don't know if I can."

"I'd say you'd have no trouble if you took another of those magic pills."

"Probably, but that medicine makes me feel like I'm having an out-of-body experience. It's not something I enjoy."

He nodded. "I'm not big on the strong pain meds either. How about some good ol' acetaminophen or ibuprofen?"

"That I'll take."

"I'll get you some." He pulled a bottle from a cabinet and tapped three gel caps into my hand.

I swallowed the meds, then walked to the windows along the back of the apartment. The moon reflected off of the snow-covered ground. "There's got to be half a foot of snow out there. That has to break some kind of October record for this part of Kentucky."

"The eleven-o'clock news predicted we'd have six to twelve inches before we're done."

I scoffed. "Don't you just love that? Six to twelve inches. If only we could all have that much latitude for accuracy in our jobs. 'Yes, Your Honor, I can say with sixty percent accuracy that I think the defendant killed the victim. I think he should get a lethal injection.'"

Luke sat on the couch and crossed his arms. "Are you a believer in the death penalty?"

I studied him. It wasn't an easy question. "I think there are too many flaws in our justice system, and too many people on death row later being proven innocent, for death to be man's decision." I lifted a finger just as Luke was about to speak. "However, if someone I loved or if a child of mine was harmed, I might change my opinion. So I guess I'm undecided."

"Did you think Ethan deserved the death penalty?" Luke asked.

I was immediately taken back to Ethan's trial. "The jury didn't think so."

"But did you?"

I turned and looked at the snow again. Clean, white, untouched. Tears threatened as I pictured Ethan's face the day of his sentencing. He was terrified. He had lost everything.

I shook my head. "No, I didn't think he deserved the death penalty." I'd had no idea why Ethan had done what he'd done, but not once did I ever believe that he had planned it.

I faced Luke again. He was rubbing his hands over his face.

"You look tired," I said. "Exhausted, actually."

He pushed away from the couch and stalked toward me. He slid a hand to my waist. "Yeah. I could use a couple more hours of sleep." He pushed a rogue strand of hair from my face. "But then I'd like to talk with you about the evidence I've accumulated upstairs."

I looked into his eyes. "I'm still a little pissed that I'm at the top of your suspect board."

"Well, I'm confident you won't be pissed after we talk.

For now, let's both get some more sleep. We'll talk about my board over breakfast and coffee."

After a deep breath in and out, I nodded. "Fine. You win."

"Good. I like winning."

THE NEXT TIME I WOKE, I wasn't alone—Luke's legs were intertwined with mine. And though I was still wearing my jeans this time, it felt too intimate for what our relationship had become after I'd seen my photograph on his wall.

I peeled my body away from his. He moaned slightly, but didn't wake up. It was still dark out, but I could see the beginnings of light on the horizon.

I went down to the kitchen and rooted around until I found coffee grounds. I was impressed by the fresh-roasted gourmet blend. Luke didn't find this at the local Paynes Creek grocery store—he must have brought it with him, or purchased it in Lexington.

I started the coffee, then roamed around the downstairs. It was definitely a cozy space. I wondered what Coop planned to do with it. Use it for guests? Rent it out? I ran my fingers along a bookshelf, past a couple of biographies, a Civil War history book, and a few suspense novels set in Kentucky, written by a local author.

When the coffee was finished, I poured myself a cup, then added milk and found some sugar in a white canister with a lid in the shape of a rooster. Armed with my coffee, I grabbed my phone from the table and curled up under a blanket on one side of the couch to check messages.

Penelope had called, then texted. Of course she'd heard about my concussion, and was checking on me. Finch had checked up on me too, late last night, and had then texted me to tell me he'd gotten a status update from Luke. He finished with: *Feel better. Call me tomorrow. Be careful. Are you sure you trust Justice?*

I knew Finch was simply showing brotherly love and support; he'd always been protective of me. But there was no reason for me not to trust Luke. He was a respected FBI agent. His only agenda was discovering the truth.

I heard Luke walking around above me, and moments later he came down the spiral staircase. "I was scared you had left," he said. "And damn it's cold." He rubbed his arms and walked over to a wood stove. Once he had it properly stoked, he faced me again. "What are you smiling at?"

I'd been watching him, but hadn't realized I was smiling. He had an air about him that reminded me of boys from college. Although he was a successful thirty-something FBI agent, he had a boyish charm that made me laugh. "I'm not sure." I looked down at my coffee, tracing the mug's rim with my finger. "You're not what I expected when I heard the FBI was getting involved."

"What did you expect?" He turned and headed for the coffee pot as if it were some beacon.

"Well, mostly I didn't care. I do my best not to get involved in the cases. I only take the pictures."

"Chief Reid thinks you can do much more than that." He poured himself a cup of coffee, then faced me again. "Says you spot details that his top detectives miss."

I shrugged. "I'm sure it helps that I'm one of the first on the scene. And that I'm the one who shoots the pictures."

"I don't think so. I'm told you have an eye. That's why the younger cops, especially those looking to be promoted to detective, are threatened by you."

"Well, that's stupid. I have no desire to be a detective.

Or any kind of police officer, for that matter." I stood, refreshed my coffee, then walked to the stairs. "On that note, I'm going up to look over your evidence board. Take your time." I started the climb to the second floor.

Luke took another sip of coffee, then said sarcastically, "For someone who doesn't want to be a detective, you seem mighty eager to look over my evidence."

I STOOD a short distance back from the evidence board so that I could take in the entire thing. On the left side was evidence related to the deaths of my mother and Eli—photos of basically every member of my family, news articles, Post-It notes, and crime scene photos. To the right were similar items related to the other arson cases—some familiar, some not. The familiar ones included photographs of Bella Reynolds and her parents, Sadie Porter and her parents, Alexandra Sims, Matthew Lake, and, to my surprise, Principal Johnson of Paynes Creek High School. I was at a loss as to how the principal might be involved.

I stayed where I was, taking sips of coffee as I stared at the board, memorizing the parts I knew something about, making mental notes and questions about the parts I didn't. I was very appreciative when Luke brought the coffee pot upstairs.

"What are you thinking?" he asked, standing next to me.

Deep in thought, I ignored him at first. I stepped closer to the board and began reading it from one side to the other. First I memorized the names on the photographs across the top—the key witnesses and victims. Then I moved down to the next row, scanning the photos of secondary characters in the stories we call crimes, the corresponding newspaper articles, and tons of Post-It notes.

"These notes are all yours?" I asked, pointing to a couple of the Post-Its.

He nodded but said nothing. He was leaning back on his heels, an arm across his chest. His other hand was still holding his mug of coffee.

There was a Post-It with the words "*Arrived in P.C. two days later?*" taped just below Finch's photo. I replayed the memory in my head of seeing Finch after that awful night so long ago. Yes, it was two days after the fire when he visited me in the hospital. Uncle Henry and Aunt Leah had been in and out, but I didn't have many other visitors. The nurses told me Ethan slept in the lobby; one nurse told me she'd seen him crying. But he never tried to enter my room. After the fire, I'd told him I never wanted to see him again.

My heart constricted at the thought. He'd been all alone. Whether he was guilty, and feeling regret over what he'd done, or innocent, and simply mourning his loss, he was alone.

Feeling suddenly weak, I grabbed hold of a chair to steady myself and set my coffee on the table, trying hard not to slosh the contents.

Luke stepped to my side. "You okay?"

"I will be. Just give me a minute."

"Is it your head? Here, sit down. If this is too much—"

"It's not. I'm fine."

"Look, you have a concussion. Have you felt nauseous? Maybe we need to follow up with your doctor this morning."

"Luke," I said, my voice taking on an edge. "I'm fine."

"Okay, but if—"

"Are you always like this? The hovering type?"

He smiled. "Not usually. I guess I'm developing a soft spot for you."

I angled my head. "Even though you know that's not a good idea?"

"Even though."

I decided now wasn't the time to talk about this temporary whatever-it-was we had going on. "Tell me about your board," I said. "I'm mostly curious about the middle—the photographs of crime scenes and people I don't recognize."

"Those are unsolved arson cases that have similarities to the night your mom died and to the three recent cases. All occurred over the past ten years."

I turned and paced back and forth in front of the cases I hadn't recognized, making mental note of the dates. "These fires occurred months, sometimes years, apart. And they occurred while Ethan was in prison." I spun around to study Luke's face. "You never thought Ethan was guilty."

"For a long time, I wasn't sure. He could have been guilty. These other cases could have been the work of a copycat—or multiple copycats. Or the similarities could have been mere coincidences. But..." He paused.

"But what?"

"Well, there are two things about your mother's murder that differentiate it from the rest of the cases. Number one, it was the first—the earliest case on my board. Number two, in all the other cases," he gestured to his wall, "the victims were murdered at a distance. Gunshot wound, carbon monoxide poisoning, drugs, the list goes on. None of them required the murderer to touch his victim. But your mother and stepfather were beaten to death. That's personal. The person who killed your mom and stepdad did so in an act of rage."

I swiped at the tears that had fallen down my cheeks.

"I'm sorry," he said

"No, go on. I can handle it."

"Okay. There's a chance we're looking at a cold, psychopathic serial killer. Perhaps your mom and Eli were his first victims, and it was personal, and after he got away with it, he kept trying to re-create that moment. And now, we have two more fires in the same town where that first fire occurred. That can't be a coincidence. So if I'm going to stop these murders, it's critical that I understand what happened all those years ago."

I looked at the wall of notes, photographs, and newspaper clippings. My eyes glided over the pictures of my mom and Ethan. I was going to be forever haunted by my memories of that night. But could I do something to stop anyone else from going through the same thing?

"How can I help?" My voice shook.

"I need you to put aside your feelings about Ethan. Pretend you're not convinced he killed your mother. I need you to walk me through the details of that night. Everything you can remember."

"You have no idea what you're asking."

"You're right. And I'm terribly sorry to put you through the pain of it. But if I'm right, there's someone out there who's been committing murders and setting fires for the past eleven years. And you can help me stop them."

TWENTY-SIX

I didn't give Luke time to stop me. I headed for the spiral staircase and went downstairs. The sun had risen and reflected brightly off of the snow, lighting the apartment, but also making the pain that lingered behind my eyes worse.

I found my snow boots by the door. My coat was hanging on a hook just inside.

"Why are you running again?" Luke asked. The calmness in his voice irritated me more than my persistent headache. "What are you afraid of?"

I stood there with my heavy coat on over his sweatshirt, my snow boots on my feet with the laces hanging loose. I was a mess. "Afraid? You think I'm afraid?"

"I know you are. And I think you want to tell me why."

I walked toward him and jabbed a finger into his chest. "You don't know shit. You certainly don't know me. And clearly you know squat about your case up there."

Before I could turn for the door, he grabbed my hand and pulled me close. His eyes stared down into mine; the heat from them threatened to overwhelm me. And I could feel his breath feather across my cheeks. "Then help me understand. Help me put a stop to these murders."

My breaths were coming fast and shallow. My chest tightened, and my head throbbed like a jackhammer. "I can't," I said weakly. "I don't know how."

"I think you do."

"You're asking too much."

"I know I am. And I'm sorry." He looked away from me for a second. When his eyes found mine again, he said, "I know about the hyperthymesia."

My eyes widened. "How?

"Chief Reid explained it to me."

Tears welled up in my eyes. "Then you know that I relive that night, along with every day before and after, over and over in my head. I don't get to shove bad memories away like most people do. I don't get to cover them with better memories. They're always there. And asking me to talk about them... it only makes it worse." I curled the fingers of my free hand into a fist and pressed that fist into my chest. "It's excruciating."

"I will be here every single second, Faith. I think if you share your story, I might be able to stop a killer. I know that won't stop you from remembering, but you'll be making sure it doesn't happen to someone else."

I let my head fall forward. "Why did they have to let Ethan out of prison?"

"Because he didn't kill your mother."

I met his gaze again. "I'm starting to realize that. And that makes this even harder. Because now I'll have to live with the guilt that I might have put him there—*and* the guilt of wishing he was *still* there."

I STARTED WITH SOMETHING EASY. There was something else I'd been keeping from Luke—about the case in Midland. I flipped through the photos from the crime scene until I found the photograph of the dog tag that identified Finch as the family's veterinarian. I tacked the photo under the newspaper articles about that case, then used twine to extend a line from this photo to the picture of Finch.

"Why didn't you mention that the first time you spotted that detail?" Luke asked.

"Family loyalty, I suppose," I said. "And I was in a bad mood that night. I had just seen Ethan at the Spotted Cat. And you were acting all superior." I let my shoulders lift and drop. "Besides, it seemed like such a tiny detail. Those tags can be found all over the state, I'm sure."

A smirk touched Luke's lips. "You don't like to help when you're having a bad day. Got it."

"Speaking of the Spotted Cat…" I went to my purse and dug out the matchbook that was left at my fire pit, lifting it carefully by the edges. "Probably no way to find fingerprints on this now."

Luke got a tissue from the nightstand and picked up the matchbook. "Doesn't hurt to process it. I'll find a plastic bag to stick this in. Write 'Spotted Cat' on a Post-It and stick it up on the board."

When he returned, I was still staring at the board.

"What are you thinking so hard about?" he asked.

"I was just noticing the dates. My mom was killed eleven and a half years ago. The next fire on your board happened more than two years later. After that, the gap of time between the fires grows tighter and tighter. The crimes are getting closer together. And now they're coming very fast. Why?"

"We noticed that too. Typically, arsonists spread their

fires far apart; they don't want to rush and get sloppy. A tighter time frame could indicate that their need for fire has become greater. But the truth is, I don't think this is about arson at all. In every one of these cases, the victims were killed prior to the fire being set—with the exception of Sadie Porter, who ran in after the fire was started. The killer couldn't have predicted that, so I believe her death was a mistake."

"You're saying you think a serial killer killed my mom and her husband." I said it aloud, then tried to process it through what I knew. "If that's true, what if Ethan and I had come home sooner than we had? Would we have been victims?"

"Maybe. Maybe not."

"Meaning?"

"There's one question you haven't asked. Possibly the biggest question in any case, especially this one."

I stared at Luke for a long moment. "Motive."

"Motive," he repeated.

TWENTY-SEVEN

"You think someone wanted my parents dead—that they had motive—but you seem certain it wasn't Ethan."

Luke nodded. "I'm certain."

"But how can you be so—" And then I understood. "You've seen the evidence. The evidence that caused the commonwealth's attorney to release Ethan and drop the case."

"I have."

I waited.

Luke took a deep breath. "Okay. Let's start with your written statement, taken three days after the fire."

I nodded. "I was in the hospital, recovering from severe burns."

"Yes. You told Chief Reid—Detective, at the time— that you had been with Ethan the night of the fire, but the two of you separated around six-thirty. You got home just after seven, and the fire was already blazing. You said that you didn't see how Ethan would have had time to leave you, get home, kill two people, and start a fire."

"But Chief told me I was wrong," I said. "He said Ethan would have had plenty of time to commit the murders and start the fire before I arrived."

"And you believed him, because you were seventeen. You'd just lost your mother and were suffering from severe burns. You were in shock. But I know you remember every single detail of that night. Look back on it now. What does your twenty-nine-year-old mind tell you?"

I drilled fingers into my forehead. "There wasn't time," I said. "He couldn't have done it. There just wasn't time."

"You're right—there wasn't. And the evidence, withheld from Ethan's attorney, proves it. There were two parts to that evidence: a witness who said they thought they saw Ethan stop at a gas station at just before seven that night, and a corresponding, time-stamped video proving it."

I couldn't believe what I was hearing. "What?"

"You testified at Ethan's trial that he pulled you from the fire. But according to the timestamp on the video…"

"There's no way he could have arrived before me and started the fire," I whispered. I fought back emotion that threatened to bubble up out of my throat.

"Tell me what really happened that night, Faith."

TWENTY-EIGHT

I managed to talk Luke into taking a walk outside. I needed the fresh air, and I craved the open space when I told him about the night my life changed forever. And maybe being outside would make me feel like I could run if I needed to. Maybe I wouldn't feel like I was being confined in the prison of my own memories, as I had been for so long.

The temperature was right around freezing, but the sun warmed our faces. Bundled up in coats, gloves, and snow boots, we walked through the woods between Coop's farm and mine. I fought against nerves and emotions. I had tried to say the words out loud so many times when I was alone, and I could never do it.

"What did Ethan do to you?" Luke asked, prompting me to begin.

I turned my head so that he couldn't see my face, but he grabbed my arm and forced me to stop.

Keeping my head pointed down at the snow, I swallowed hard. Then I took a deep breath and squared my shoulders. I lifted my eyes to Luke's and said the words that I'd only said to one other person.

"He raped me."

Unwelcome tears stung my eyes, but I blinked them away before they stung my cold cheeks.

"My stepbrother—my best friend—got drunk and forced himself on me."

If Luke had a reaction, he did an incredible job of suppressing it. "Who knew about it?"

"No one," I said, then started walking again. I couldn't bear to watch the pity form in Luke's eyes. Whether he'd wanted it to be there or not, I knew it was. "Not then anyway. Later, I told one of my therapists."

"Wait a minute." He stopped me again. "You never told your family that Ethan sexually assaulted you?"

"Nope. Not back then, and not since."

"What about your therapist? Did they suggest you tell the authorities?"

"Ethan was already behind bars with a life sentence by the time I told her. So no, she didn't push me to report it. What would be the point?"

Luke grabbed me and pulled me to him. He wrapped his strong arms around me, and he hugged me tightly against him. "I'm so sorry for what you've been through."

Even through our winter coats, I could feel the comfort he was offering me. I was rigid at first, but when I realized he wasn't going to let go, I relaxed into his hold. But I refused to shed a single tear. I'd shed enough tears.

Eventually, Luke did release me. We walked in silence for several minutes. Then Luke began asking questions I knew he needed to ask.

"Would Ethan have told anyone?"

"I don't know," I said. "No one has ever mentioned it. People did speculate that he and I carried on a secret relationship when we were in high school, though; they whispered about us behind our backs, and sometimes right to our faces." I thought of Bella and Alexandra in the park.

"Your brother never knew? Your aunt or uncle?"

"My brother was off at college. I don't see how my aunt or my uncle would have known."

"Was this a one-time occurrence?" Luke asked, then immediately said, "I am so sorry to ask you this. God, I wish I didn't need to know."

"That night was the first time he actually forced himself on me, but he had tried to convince me that we were meant to be together many times. He was convinced that he was in love with me, and that since we weren't related by blood, we should be able to be together."

"I assume he thought you had feelings for him?"

"He knew I loved him. But as a brother and best friend. I never wanted it to be anything more than that. And because of my love for him, I was blinded to how deep his feelings for me ran. I never believed he would hurt me."

"Of course you didn't." This time when Luke spoke, I heard anger in his voice. "You trusted him."

"I did." A lump formed in my throat. The memories were so fresh—as they always were—and those old feelings washed over me, forcing tears despite my desperate objections.

I began to shake. I fell to my knees. And I sobbed.

Luke was behind me. He, too, went to his knees, and he hugged me from behind, letting me cry without abandon, my body heaving through a bout of wrenching sobs. "I am so sorry," he said. "You've kept this bottled up long enough. You'll feel better if you let it all out."

But he didn't get it. With hyperthymesia—even with the amount of therapy I'd been through—nothing could make me feel better. I could never stop from feeling the memories, at full strength, every time they came to my mind.

"Let me get you back to Coop's," he said.

"I want to go home," I managed. We were already closer to my trailer at that point.

He helped me up, and I managed to hold in further sobs as we walked. But I knew the dam I'd constructed wouldn't hold. I would have to cry over the grief of losing my mom—and the grief of being violated by my best friend. I would cry at having the last vestiges of my youth ripped violently away. I would cry until I had no tears left.

I TRIED to convince Luke to leave when we reached my trailer, but he refused, and with my throbbing head, I didn't have the energy to argue with him. I went straight to my bed while Luke made himself comfortable in the front of the trailer. I thought I heard him talking on the phone, but I simply buried my head deeper into my pillow.

And when the well of tears eventually dried up, I realized that I felt something—felt more than I wanted to—for this man who refused to leave me alone even after I'd confided in him about the single worst night of my life.

I knew he could have coerced me to tell that story sooner than he had. He had clearly known there was more to my story—had known I was hiding something. And he had *needed* to know what I knew. It was the only way to stop these murders. Yet he had been patient.

Was it truly possible that a serial killer had been on a rampage for more than a decade—and that they had started with my mother and stepfather? That some psychopath had set the fire that had scarred my body and changed my life?

Several hours passed. I could tell the sun was low in the sky by the light in my bedroom, and the chill inside my trailer. I rolled out of bed and wrapped myself in a large sweater. I could hear the banging of pots and pans in the kitchen. As I pulled open the divider, I smiled at the thought of Luke making me something to eat.

But it wasn't Luke standing in my trailer. It was my brother.

I frowned. "What are you doing here?"

"It's good to see you, too," he said. "I'm making us some spaghetti. It was either that or tacos. It's all I really know how to make. How are you feeling?"

"Better. Where's Luke?" I looked past Finch as if Luke could be hiding in the hundred square feet of space beyond the kitchen.

"He got called in to work. He didn't want to leave you alone, so he called me. I had a surgery cancel today, so I took off early. I wanted to see how my kid sister was doing anyway. Luke said he pushed you to talk about the night Mom died. Said he was pretty rough on you."

"It's fine. Just dredged up all the memories, you know?"

"Well, I know how it is for me. I can't even imagine how it is for you."

Finch had seen me break down over too many memories at once. He knew life was hard for me, even if he couldn't imagine what it was like to remember your worst memories like they were happening again. Of course, Finch thought I was only remembering the fire, and Mom's death. He had no idea what Ethan had done to me.

"Finch," I said, hesitantly. I didn't want to make him have to relive that horrific time. "How did you manage to finish college after that?"

He stirred the sauce on the stove, then looked over at me. "The same way you managed to get through high school, I guess. We both did what we had to do. And having Aubrey helped. But she was dealing with so much of her own stuff then."

I didn't know what he meant by that, but I didn't press. "Aunt Leah made it easier for me. She literally did everything for me." She went out and purchased me new clothes that would cover my bandages and scars. She made every meal, never asking for help, and she didn't let me help when I offered. She made sure I answered every college letter that spring, and encouraged me to accept the proffered scholarship into the forensics program at Eastern Kentucky University.

"She and Uncle Henry helped me a lot, too," Finch said. "I don't know what I would have done without them. And I was so thankful they could help you. I was ready to give up vet school to take care of you, but Uncle Henry and Aunt Leah wouldn't hear of it. I guess they forced us both to stand on our own two feet and not let our tragedy define us."

"I guess," I said. When the water in the second pot was boiling, I reached for the box of spaghetti and dumped some in. "Thanks for coming over. I know you hate cooking in this tiny kitchen."

He smiled. "It's not so bad." He looked around. "You've done pretty well for yourself. This place suits you."

I glanced around to see what he was seeing. "Yeah. It's fine for now."

"So… the FBI agent?" Finch asked.

"How long have you been saving that question?"

"Since yesterday when we were at Uncle Henry and Aunt Leah's. I don't like him. And I'm surprised that you trust him. He's digging a little too deeply into our pasts."

"He's just doing his job."

"Do you care for him?"

I shrugged. "Too early to tell."

"I don't know," he sang. "Aubrey and I knew after our first date that we would be going on many, many more."

"Well, that's you and Aubrey. You two are different. You have something really special."

"Oh, and you can't find something special?" He drew back. "Not that I'm saying it should be this jerk."

I laughed, then picked up a slotted spoon and played with the softening noodles. "I don't know. That kind of love might not be in the cards for me. Can you imagine being in a relationship with me? I remember every bad thing anyone has ever said or done to me. And I hold grudges. There's no way to win a fight with me."

"True." He pulled a couple of plates from an overhead cabinet. "Seriously, though—how much do you trust this guy? He did say he was rough on you today—though to his credit, he seemed torn up about it."

"It was necessary. And he had to ask."

"Why? That was over ten years ago."

"Because the FBI doesn't think Ethan was responsible for Mom's death." I took the plates and set them on my dining table.

He gripped the stirring spoon so hard that his knuckles turned white. "And you believe him?"

I was quiet for a moment, then I met his hard stare. "I do, Finch. Ethan isn't completely innocent, but he wasn't responsible for either the murders or the fire." I didn't want to get into what Ethan was guilty of. Not yet.

"So they're pushing forward with the reopening of the investigation? That's what today was all about? That's why he's digging up the past?" He closed his eyes and took in a deep breath. "Son of a bitch. He had no right."

"He had every right. I'm just thankful he questioned me as gently as he could. Any other investigator would have grilled me harder. At least Luke could take me home and let me curl up in bed after."

"I guess I should thank him for that." Finch eyed me sideways. "I won't, but I know I should."

I nudged him playfully with my hip. "Do what you do best and be nice. Let him do his job. If what he told me today is true, they're looking for a serial killer. And serial arsonist."

"Wow. So they think these recent fires are linked to Mom's murder." There was something in Finch's voice. It wasn't disbelief. He seemed to be analyzing something of his own.

I nodded. "And there have been more, in other places. But the pieces of the puzzle seem to be clicking into place." I shrugged. "At least Luke seems to think so."

"And does he think all this is connected to you getting hit in the head last night? Or is he convinced, like the rest of us, that was Ethan getting revenge?"

"Revenge?" I said.

"Well, if he thinks he was wrongly imprisoned, he must blame you—for not helping him stay out of prison in the first place."

I thought about that for a second. *Was* I to blame for Ethan's wrongful imprisonment? If so, he was the obvious suspect for stalking me. "I have no idea."

We served spaghetti onto our plates and sat across from each other to eat. My mind was racing with so many unanswered questions. Some days I wished I could hook up my trailer to my large SUV and drive away from Paynes Creek for good. But as I looked at Finch—and as I thought of Aubrey and their unborn child—I knew I could never leave my family behind.

I closed my eyes tightly and swallowed back heavy emotions. I would not cry again. The earlier episode had left me raw, and I simply refused to add to it. Not that it was always within my control.

Instead I took a bite of spaghetti, savoring the Italian spices and garlic in the sauce.

We made idle chitchat while we ate. But my mind wasn't in it. In the brief moments of silence, I couldn't help but think about the things Luke and I had discussed. After all these years, had someone uncovered what Ethan had done to me?

The current murders—if that's what they were, and I believed they were—all involved people who knew about the abuse of someone they loved. Sandra and Gordon Reynolds knew about Matthew Lake's inappropriate relationship with their daughter well before they elected to press charges against him. And Sadie Porter's parents knew about Matthew Lake's transgressions, too—though they kept it to themselves, apparently in the hope that their daughter might get an opportunity at Juilliard.

And… Ethan and I had had a relationship that many would have thought was inappropriate. But even if someone had found out about that now, who could possibly have known about it back then? And who would have cared enough to do something about it? We had been so careful.

If my case was anything like the Reynoldses' and the Porters'… did that mean my mother knew about Ethan and me? Had she and Eli *both* known?

And if so, had someone killed them for it?

FINCH WOULDN'T LEAVE until Luke returned. He claimed

that he just wanted to visit with me, but it didn't make sense that he would leave Aubrey on her own this long. And when I pressed harder, he admitted that they'd had an argument. "I accused her of not putting our child's needs ahead of her own," he said.

I knew the doctor had ordered her to stay in bed, and she was resisting it. "Do you mean because she's not resting enough?" I asked.

"It's worse than that. She went out driving around last night. You saw the condition of the roads."

"Why would she leave in the middle of a snowstorm?"

"She went to Walmart." Finch laughed. "Said she just browsed around the baby department mesmerized by all the things we would need when our baby arrives."

"Well... I'm sure she's not still angry with you," I said. "And if she's refusing to stay in bed, you really should be there, don't you think?"

"It's okay. I had Aunt Leah stop by and check on her. She took Aubrey some chicken noodle soup and watched some television with her."

"Well, I appreciate you coming over. It's annoying that I needed you, but I'm thankful."

And I was thankful—but I also knew Luke didn't want me left alone. That was kind of cute, but mostly, it irritated me. I didn't take well to being babied. I supposed, though, that since someone had managed to give me a nice knot on the back of my head and a concussion, I didn't have a lot of room to argue.

Luke took over babysitting duties at nine p.m. I gave Finch a hug before he left.

When the door was closed behind him, I turned to Luke—who was already closing the distance between us.

"I am so sorry about earlier," he said. "I'm sorry I had

to put you through that, and I'm sorry I had to leave right after."

I wriggled out of his embrace. "It's fine. I'm fine. You were just doing your job." The sarcasm spilled into my voice before I could stop it.

"Ouch."

I shrugged. The truth sometimes hurt. "Sorry." I pulled some over-the-counter painkillers from a cabinet and popped three.

"Head still hurt?" he asked—trying, and failing, to hide his disappointment.

"Yeah, but it just feels like a normal tension headache now. I don't feel the need for the stronger meds." I faced Luke again. "I need to go see Ethan."

Luke's brows pointed inward. "Why?"

"He and I once had what I thought was an unbreakable bond. And I know we can never go back to what was once a wonderful brother-sister relationship—he ruined that forever—but when he came to me last week, he apologized for hurting me. And… I need to forgive him. Not for him… but for me."

"You're a much better person than I, then. Because I've had a lot of ideas about what I'd like to do to him, and none of those ideas involve forgiveness."

I smiled, then stepped to Luke and placed a hand on his face. "I've been thinking about the fact that Ethan has spent more than ten years in a state penitentiary with little hope of getting out. If instead of murder and arson, he had been convicted of raping me…"

"He'd gotten four to five years, maybe," Luke said.

I scoffed. "He would have gotten a slap on the wrist—at most."

"You think so?"

I closed my eyes for a moment. I didn't want to fall

apart again. And I had no desire to tell Luke more about my teenage relationship with Ethan. "I've played out the 'what ifs' a billion times, and almost every time, my baseball star stepbrother walks free. We were best friends, and we were rumored to be more than that. The town loved to gossip about us. A decent attorney would easily have proven reasonable doubt. He would have said we were both drunk, which was true. That we'd had consensual sex. And that I later regretted it because he was my stepbrother, and that I called it rape out of guilt. My reputation would have been ruined. It's always the girl's reputation that's ruined."

I shook my head and looked up into Luke's eyes. "Our relationship is complicated, for sure. But I have to forgive him if I'm ever to let go of some of this hate I have pent up." I placed a fist over my heart.

Luke eyed me. Several beats passed before he said, "Okay. I'll allow it."

I pulled back. "You'll 'allow' it? I wasn't asking permission. I was just telling you my plans as a courtesy, so that when one of the agents you have following me or Ethan spots the meeting, you won't be surprised."

"How did you know—"

"That you have agents following me? Please. I told you I didn't care if you put someone at the end of my driveway. The question is: Is the agent here to protect me or to spy on me?"

Luke lifted a brow. "Why would you think my agent would be here to spy on you?"

"Please." I crossed my arms. "Don't patronize me. I know how this case looks. And my photograph is still at the top of your evidence board."

"As a person of interest. Along with a lot of people.

Like your brother, who you yourself linked to the Midland case."

"I didn't 'link' him, I just pointed out a dog tag!" My voice rose an octave, and I quickly turned and began messing with Gus's food and water bowls. I knew when the Midland fire happened, and thanks to my condition, I knew every detail of my day and night—including the fact that Finch was out of town. But I wasn't about to mention that to Luke, and have him start harassing my brother.

Luke was watching me, analyzing me for sure. "There's something you're not telling me."

I rolled my eyes. "Don't be ridiculous. Why would I keep something from you?" I had already shared with him my biggest secret.

"That's exactly what I'm wondering. But I know what it looks like for someone to busy themselves so that they don't have to make eye contact with an interrogator."

"Is that what this is? An interrogation?"

He sighed. "Of course not. But that doesn't change the fact that you're hiding something."

"Well, hotshot FBI agent, I'm sure you'll figure it out. Now, are you staying here tonight or going home, because I need to get ready for bed."

I tried to edge past him. I was tired, and my head ached. But he boxed me against my kitchen counter.

"I don't know what just happened, Faith, but you went into your shell well before you got upset about me leaving your picture at the top of my board. What's going on?"

"What else do you want from me? I helped you prove that you can link my mom's murder to all your other cases. Congratulations, Agent. You've got yourself a serial killer. Now, if you don't mind, I want you to leave. I'm still feeling the effects of a concussion, and I'd like to get some sleep."

"That's fine. I'll let you push me away. Because you're right, I do want to solve this case. But don't think for one second you'll be pushing me away forever. This thing between us..." He motioned between us with the wave of a finger. "We'll see it through eventually."

He held my stare for several beats. I thought he might lean in and kiss me, and I couldn't say I would have pushed him away if he did. But instead he turned, and I watched him walk out of my trailer without another word.

TWENTY-NINE

The next day, forty-five minutes after ducking out the back entrance of the police station—and losing my FBI tail in the process—I was sitting at a booth inside a fifties-style diner on the north side of Lexington.

Ten minutes after that, Ethan walked in wearing jeans and a navy pullover. He hadn't lost his casual style or his boy-next-door good looks behind bars, but he'd developed a few extra lines around his eyes and had filled out across the chest. He'd obviously bulked up while he was in prison.

I scanned the parking lot for any sign of a tail.

As he approached the table, he followed my nervous glance outside. "What is it? Are you being followed?"

"I ditched my tail. I was looking for yours."

As he slid into the booth across from me, he laughed. "I've ditched those fools every day this week." When our eyes met again, his brows furrowed, shadowing his eyes. "How are you?" he asked. "Is your head okay?"

My hand went instinctively to the back of my neck. The knot was still tender. "I'm fine."

A waitress interrupted us, and I ordered a diet soda; Ethan ordered unsweetened tea.

"Do they have any idea who's doing these things to you?" Ethan asked when the waitress was gone.

"Yes." I narrowed my gaze. "You."

"Figures they wouldn't try to find any other suspects." There was anger in his voice.

"Why were you out at my trailer? I told you to leave me alone."

He folded his hands on the table between us. "I don't know. I was out driving, and I found myself in Paynes Creek. That farm meant something to me once upon a time. Still does."

"Then why were you so quick to give it up?"

"You think I let go of that farm easily?"

I glanced down at my fidgety hands. "No, I guess not."

"I want you to have the farm. I hope you'll eventually purchase Finch's share, too. If that's what you want."

"Where are you living?"

"In the back of my bar."

My eyes dropped to a knife mark left on the surface of the table. "I'm sorry."

"What are you sorry for?"

"I don't know." Frustration coated my words. "I just think I'm supposed to be sorry."

"You have nothing to be sorry for. I'm the one who hurt you." He paused a few beats. "But don't you think I've paid for my crime?"

I lifted my eyes. "What do you mean by that?"

"Even with a horrible attorney and a ruthless judge, I would never have gotten eleven years for what I did to you. I've served my time."

I thought back to the first night he showed up uninvited to my land. "Is that what you meant when you said you did it for me?"

The waitress set our drinks in front of us, and Ethan shooed her away, telling her we would let her know if we decided to order food.

I leaned forward when she was gone. "I'm supposed to believe that you willingly went to prison just because you felt you deserved it? Not for the murder and arson, but for the rape? That you made sure you got out when your time was up?" I leaned back. "And what? I'm supposed to forgive you now?"

He didn't answer. He only pleaded with me with his warm blue eyes—eyes that reminded me of hot summer nights. In high school, we had spent many such nights lying under the stars, dreaming of what we would be when we left Paynes Creek. I knew then that Ethan had eyes that could win over any girl he wanted. Yet he spent all his time hanging out with me, uninterested in other girls.

I'd told Luke that I was requesting this meeting with Ethan so that I could forgive him. But that wasn't true. I was unsure if I could ever forgive the rapist now sitting across from me. No one knew how difficult it was for me to even face this man. Not Luke. Certainly not Ethan. And apart from them, and one therapist, no one else even knew what had happened.

At least... that's what I had thought.

"I have to ask you something," I said. I let my gaze wander outside again. It was difficult to maintain eye contact with Ethan.

"You can ask me anything."

"Did you tell anyone about that night? About what you did to me?"

Ethan's eyes widened. "Never in a million years!" He reached across the table and grabbed one of my hands

207

before I could jerk it away. "I knew right afterwards that I had screwed up. I've tried so many times to tell you how sorry I was for what I did—that it was one hundred percent my fault. I wrote you hundreds of letters over the years, but they never seemed good enough, so I just shredded them and flushed them down the toilet. But I never told anyone else."

Why I allowed him to continue to hold my hand, I wasn't sure. His fingers were calloused and rough. But his skin was cool and his touch gentle as he rubbed his thumb against the top of my hand. It took me back to when we were best friends—when I saw him as my brother.

"Did you ever tell anyone about *other* things that we did?" I asked. Sweat broke out across my shoulders and extended down my arms to my hands, and I pulled my hand back.

"Why are you asking these things, Faith? Look, I was in love with you. I knew you couldn't handle that idea, but I never gave up hope that you would someday accept that we were good for each other. And no, of course I never told anyone."

"What happened after you left me that night?" I asked. "Where did you go, if not home?"

"So, you finally want to know my side of the story?" His frustration showed in his eyes.

I didn't answer. I just waited.

He sighed. "I'll tell you what happened, but not here."

I RELUCTANTLY FOLLOWED Ethan through the Spotted Cat into a back room. "You realize the FBI is out in your parking lot, right?" I asked.

Luke had probably received a phone call already, and

now knew I was here. He might already be on his way. I understood he was just trying to keep me safe; he still felt Ethan was most likely the person who had assaulted me. But I hoped he didn't arrive too quickly. I needed to hear Ethan's story.

"They never seem to leave," Ethan said. "I lose them, and they just come back here and wait for me to return. I'm learning to live with it. I've got my attorney on speed dial in case they overstep or outstay their welcome. It's not like the police didn't pin me for a crime I didn't commit once already. But I'm watching my step."

Either Ethan was extremely arrogant, or he really wasn't involved in any of the recent crimes.

The back room of the Spotted Cat had been converted into a living area. There was a leather sofa, a coffee table with stacks of books, an old rolltop desk with lots of paper strewn about, and a single bed. "So you really are living here," I said. I didn't mean for it to sound judgmental, but it did.

"For now. While I get on my feet. It's not easy— everyone around here knows my face, and they all decided I was guilty long ago. I applied for a few jobs before buying this place, with no luck. I'm not even qualified to be a dish- washer, apparently."

"Why did you buy this particular place?"

Ethan shrugged. "I don't know. It was for sale. It's close to Paynes Creek, but far enough that I can start over. I was pretty good at running the prison kitchen. And I studied a bartending book while in prison. Just for fun, you know. And I think I could make something of this place eventu- ally. I already have some regulars. And every once in a while a talented band shows up. I figure it'll be a slow build, but I have time now."

I pressed my hand to my heart, thinking about him

hitting certain milestones while in prison—his eighteenth birthday, his twenty-first birthday, the anniversary of his father's death. I wanted to hate him; I still feared him. But for some reason, my heart ached when I thought about how alone he had been.

"Most people fight like hell to get out of Paynes Creek," I said. "Why would you, of all people, want to stay close?"

His eyes held mine. "Because you're still here."

I didn't move for several long moments, didn't speak.

He let out an uncomfortable laugh. "If you could see the look on your face. How terrified you are."

My phone buzzed in my pocket. I jumped at the vibration, but I didn't move. Just stared at Ethan, considering.

"You going to get that?"

I pulled the phone out and looked at the screen. A call from Luke. "No, it's nothing."

"Nothing? Or is it your friend, the FBI agent?"

"You said you would tell me what happened. So…?" I needed to get his story before Luke got here. Ethan certainly wouldn't talk after Luke showed up.

"Right," he said. He walked to the rolltop desk, shuffled through some papers, and came up with a key. He knelt in front of a safe on the floor, unlocked it, and pulled out a manila folder. "The commonwealth's attorney stopped fighting me when I proved, through my attorney, that they'd withheld exculpatory evidence."

"Luke told me about the gas station video. I'm sorry, Ethan; I swear I never knew."

"No one but the prosecution and the cops could have known," he said. "But that's not all. The prosecution also didn't turn over some of the crime scene photos—photos they decided had no impact on the case against me."

"They didn't have the right to decide that," I said.

"Funny—that was my reaction as well. And, conveniently it seems to me, when I hired a new attorney for the appeal, he was told by both the prosecution and by the Paynes Creek PD that the crime scene photos had gone missing."

"Gone missing?" I thought of the photos I kept in a box at my trailer. Had I stolen the only copy?

"Apparently there was a glitch in the system where the photos were stored. They claimed that since digital photography was still so new, they were working out kinks in their storage methods and lost a whole year's worth of images."

I cocked my head. "That's bullshit. Most entities have been operating with digital photography since the early 2000s."

"Well, anyway, the digital files were lost. Deliberately, I believe."

"So how did you get these?"

"Because the prosecutor lied. They may have deleted the digital files, but they kept a physical copy. And a secretary dug them up and sent them to me."

"Why would some secretary risk her job to do such a thing?"

"Do you remember Tabitha Green? She went to middle school with us, but transferred to a school in Lexington when we were freshmen?"

"Yes. I didn't like her."

"Right. Well, she didn't like you either, and she believed you were responsible for my conviction. Apparently she followed my case closely over the years. She actually believed that you conspired with Uncle Henry to plant enough evidence to make me look guilty. She also knew I'd gotten saddled with a court-appointed attorney who didn't know his ass from his face. So she sent me everything—the photos, the statement of the witness who saw me at the gas station, the time-stamped video. For the first time since I'd been incarcerated, I had hope."

I looked away briefly.

"Everyone seems to have forgotten that I lost a parent that night, too," he continued. "Not to mention everything else that mattered to me. But I haven't forgotten. And no one wants to find the real killer more than me."

He handed the folder to me.

I flipped through the photos one by one, fighting back the bile that threatened when I saw my mother's and Eli's charred bodies. There were photos of the remains of the house. There were shots of Ethan's car, my car, and the insides of both vehicles. There were photos of the inside of the barn, and of the area around the fire pit.

But I had seen all this before.

Then I flipped to the last photo.

"What is this? I've never seen this photo before."

I lifted my head, studied Ethan's expression. It wasn't smug, but it was confident—like he knew I would finally accept that he was one hundred percent innocent. But there was also sadness in his eyes.

The photo showed what was left of one of the walls. It was damaged from fire and smoke, but some of the white shiplap showed through, and a set of decorative hooks had survived—the hooks where the family always hung their keys when they entered the house.

I let my fingers roam softly over the photograph. I traced the keys that hung on the hooks: Mom's, Eli's... "Your keys aren't there," I whispered, though I knew that meant nothing. Not really.

"Because I didn't come home until after you—after the fire was already out of control. You were running inside the house when I arrived." Ethan shuddered at the memory. "But that's not the point."

I looked up, stared at him while replaying the scene inside my head and trying to see it from his point of view. I held up a finger just as he started to say something else. "I just want to make sure I've got this straight. You'd been drinking. You'd just forced yourself on me. You left me at the school, and then you... went to a gas station? Why?"

He closed his eyes as I spoke, regret washing over his face. When he opened his eyes, he inched toward me just slightly, and I resisted the urge to step back. "Yes, *we'd* been drinking. I'd just done a horrible thing—a thing that will haunt me for the rest of my life. And..." he lifted his shoulders, "I needed gas."

"You needed gas."

"Yes. I needed gas, as pedestrian as that sounds. And that need for gas was the only thing that prevented me from arriving home before you... and possibly saving our parents' lives. I don't know."

"Or maybe the choice to stop for gas was what saved you from being killed too." My voice lowered to a whisper.

"Maybe. But take another look at the photo. You're missing something very important."

I looked at the photo again. There was another item hanging on one of the hooks. "A dog leash." We didn't have a dog, but I immediately recognized the leash. My heart rate sped up "I don't understand," I said weakly.

Ethan placed a hand on my arm. "I think you do."

I shook my head. "What you're saying can't be true." But even I heard the disbelief in my voice.

"You and I both know that Aunt Leah and Uncle Henry sometimes came over with Scout, their crazy border collie, and when they did, they always hung the leash there. This proves that one of them was there that night—*and* that they left in a hurry, because they wouldn't have left without the leash otherwise. It could have been either one of them, but one of them is the fire chief. And who better to know how to commit arson, then plant evidence to make it look like someone else had done it?"

I looked down. What Ethan was saying scared me—but he was only half right. And he was wrong about the most important point.

That's not Scout's leash.

The leash hanging on the hook was brown leather, with a handle that had been needlepointed in navy, featuring small brown dogs with orange collars. I recognized that leash. Aunt Leah had made it. She'd been into needlepointing back then, and she liked to give belts, key chains, and other items as gifts. We'd all received a handmade gift the previous Christmas.

My hand began to shake as I touched the photograph of the leash. "I don't understand," I said again. I stumbled slightly. Ethan held tighter to my arm, steadying me, then helped me to the leather sofa.

"Listen, I know Henry and Leah were there for you after the fire. And I have no idea why Henry would hurt our parents. But he *was* there that night. I'm sure of it."

I couldn't speak. I had no words for what Ethan was suggesting. Or for what I saw in the photo. "This is a lie. You're putting thoughts in my head that are impossible." There was little conviction behind my words.

Ethan sat next to me. I flinched when our knees touched, so he scooted away just slightly. "Look at me, Faith."

I kept my head down. I didn't want to look at Ethan; I couldn't. That leash should have given the police another person to investigate. But they didn't. All the other evidence pointed at Ethan, and they never considered anyone else.

"Faith." Ethan slowly reached his hand to my cheek

and turned my head. "Look at me."

I lifted my head, studying the intent expression on his face.

"I did not kill our parents. But someone did. And someone is threatening your safety now. I don't know if they're the same people, but I want to help you find out … if you'll let me. Henry knows more than he's told you. He was there that night. And for whatever reason, I think he deliberately steered the arson investigation to point to me."

"And once the police believed you had started the fire…"

"It wasn't that big of a step to pin the murders on me."

I stared at him for three more seconds, then stood abruptly. "No. This photograph means nothing. Uncle Henry wouldn't have kept information from authorities. He's a good man."

Ethan stood as well, toe to toe with me. He was a full head taller. "Okay. Let's say you're right. But can you now at least admit that I did not murder our parents? And having admitted that, you have to wonder who *did*—and who's stalking you now."

I shook my head. "Just because the story from that night is complicated, doesn't mean you're not the one who's tormenting me now."

"You don't believe that."

"I have to go." I grabbed my coat and my purse. "Can I take this?" I held up the photo.

He nodded. "Please don't run out angry like this."

I had my hand wrapped around the doorknob when he spoke again.

"I'm here for you when you realize I'm right. And I'm not going anywhere. I will prove to you how sorry I am, and that I'm not the one who ruined your life. We *can* be a family again."

THIRTY

My tires spun along a patch of ice as I raced out of the Spotted Cat parking lot. The wet roads had frozen over again as the temperature dropped. But I would face my uncle tonight. I would force him to tell me the truth. There *had* to be an explanation for what was in that photo. And for why Ethan had been charged with a crime he clearly did not commit.

I did my best to watch out for the slick spots as I drove, but I was angry and distracted. I squeezed the steering wheel, my knuckles whitening. And I remembered…

I remembered that night so clearly. How the fire shot from the windows when I drove down the driveway. The crime scene photos showed that I had left my car door open.

I had believed that Ethan was already home, because that's what the investigators told me in the hospital two days later. But that wasn't part of my actual memory. I didn't see his car, because my attention was entirely on the flames. I just sprinted from my car and into the house without thinking. My memory told me nothing about Ethan's presence, one way or the other.

When I spotted Mom on the kitchen floor, I screamed for her to get up. I kneeled next to her, begged her to wake up and get out of the house. I was in shock—from the events of the evening or from seeing my mother and Eli trapped inside our burning home, I wasn't sure. But she and Eli both just lay there, lifeless. Eli's face was swollen and bloody, and my mother's head lay in a pool of blood. Investigators would convince me later that Mom and Eli had been beaten by Ethan in a fit of rage.

Even as flames leapt to my jacket, I stood firm, yelling at my mother and coughing from too much smoke. I fought every flight instinct, forcing my body to ignore my mind's desperate pleas, accepting that I would die before leaving my mother's side. Between what Ethan had done to me and the sight of my mother's lifeless body, I simply didn't care.

And then Ethan circled his arms around me, not caring that the fire would kill him, too.

But the fire didn't kill either of us. He carried me from the burning house like I weighed nothing. He smothered the flames on my clothing with his own jacket, and he held me until fire trucks and an ambulance arrived.

He repeated so many times as we lay in the dirt, "I'm sorry. I'm so sorry."

Over the years, I never knew which part he regretted most. Raping me, or killing our parents?

Now I knew.

On this cold, icy night, as I neared my uncle's house with these fresh memories on my mind, my body shook. Uncle Henry had lied. There was no other explanation. He had to have known Ethan was innocent—and yet he pointed the authorities at Ethan anyway. And he did it to save someone else.

But what if Uncle Henry denied everything? What proof did I have?

I pulled over to the side of the road to process my thoughts. I needed a better plan than to just run in with accusations that would ruin our family forever. Maybe I was stalling, but I wanted to be sure. I wanted the rest of the crime scene photos I had taken from Uncle Henry all those years ago. I would confront Uncle Henry with all of the evidence I had and with the photos of the victims I'd stolen from him.

I turned my vehicle around.

It was dark, and the clouds covering the moon and stars made it even darker out on these country roads with no street lamps to light the way. The rain had turned to freezing rain; the road was getting covered in ice. And less than a mile from home, I fishtailed. The back end of my vehicle began sliding faster than the front end, and I spun out of control. Fortunately, no one else was on the road. Unfortunately, I spun into a ditch. I was already suffering from a concussion, and I couldn't imagine the additional jolt helped—but I was otherwise unharmed.

I tried to pull back onto the road, but it was no use— my tires just spun. I was stuck.

On the verge of tears from frustration, anger, and fear, I pulled out my phone. My first instinct was to call Uncle Henry. I knew he or someone from the station would be able to pull me out. But I simply couldn't call him, not under the circumstances. And I couldn't call Finch, either. What would I say to him? Just come out and tell him what the photo suggested?

What I should do is call the police. They'd send someone

out to help me. But I couldn't stop thinking about Chief Reid's role in the case against Ethan all those years ago. He was the lead investigator on the case; how could he not have known about all the exculpatory evidence? The gas station video, the witness, the photo? Yet he had been the one who had explained to me, who had convinced me, how it was possible that Ethan had had time to commit the murders.

I scrolled through my phone and dialed.

Luke answered on the first ring. "Are you okay? Why did you ditch the officers I had on you? They're only there to protect—"

"Can you come get me?"

He must have sensed the desperation in my voice, because his tone changed immediately. "I'm on my way. Where?"

"On the side of the road." I described where I was, and promised to leave my parking lights on.

I could hear him getting in his SUV. "I'm on my way. Want to tell me what you were thinking by ditching your protection?"

I leaned my head against the headrest and closed my eyes. "No."

"What if he had hurt you again?"

I sighed. "Just come get me before someone crashes into me." I hung up.

I knew he'd just been trying to keep me on the line to make sure I was safe as he drove, but I didn't want to talk to him about Ethan. Of *course* I'd ditched my tail before meeting with him; Ethan wouldn't have talked to me otherwise. He didn't trust the police, and why would he? The police had put him in prison once already—wrongly—and he'd lost eleven years of his life.

I wondered what kind of person Ethan would have

become if that hadn't happened. Would I still hate him the way I do now?

I *did* still hate him, didn't I?

He'd ruined me in so many ways. And then he left me to grieve for my mother alone. Sure, I had Finch, but he was away at school, and he remained distant for years after the incident, not coming home from vet school very often.

I'd felt deserted. If it hadn't been for Uncle Henry and Aunt Leah…

Headlights flashed against the back of my closed eyelids.

Luke had gotten to me quickly.

"Wonderful weather we're having this year," he said as he helped me out.

I rolled my eyes.

A gentleman, Luke walked me to the passenger side of his SUV. "Should I call for a tow truck?"

I looked back at my SUV. It was farther off the road than I'd thought—little chance of anyone crashing into it. "I'll do it in the morning. It's not going anywhere."

He got behind the wheel. "Where to?"

"My place."

He pulled back onto the road. "You gonna tell me what Ethan had to say?"

I stared straight ahead. "Eventually." I knew I needed to trust Luke, and I would. But as painful as it would be, I needed to be sure first.

Luke was quiet the rest of the way. As he pulled to a stop in front of my trailer, he finally broke the silence. "I could charge you with obstruction of justice."

I closed my eyes, attempting to come up with a way to stall him. Deciding I needed to keep things as lighthearted as I could, I turned in my seat. "You could. But then I would never sleep with you again." I intended to say that with a touch of humor, though I heard none in my voice.

"Is that an invitation?" As he asked the question, his gaze fixed on my trailer. His jaw hardened, and he reached for his weapon. "Stay here."

"What? Why——" And then I saw what he had. My trailer door stood wide open.

He climbed out of the vehicle and, keeping his gun pointed toward the ground, walked toward my trailer.

"Shit," I said, getting out and following him.

"FBI!" Luke announced. "Come out nice and slow. Show me your hands."

My trailer was as dark as the night sky, and the only sounds were Luke and me breathing.

"Get the flashlight from my glove box," Luke ordered.

I ran back to the vehicle and retrieved a Maglite. He took it, shined it into the trailer, then stepped slowly up the steps. "I'm coming in! And I will shoot first and ask questions later."

I listened for any sounds, including the sound of Gus. My heart thumped loudly in my chest as I waited for the all-clear from Luke.

He appeared in the doorway several seconds later. "It's empty, but the place is a mess."

While Luke called it in, I shouted for Gus. "Gus, I've got some fish with your name on it!" I had promised Gus a long time ago that I would never say, "Here, kitty, kitty." She just didn't seem like the type of cat that would enjoy being treated like a wimpy little kitten her whole life.

When Luke hung up, he helped me look for Gus. He pointed his flashlight under the trailer and yelled for Gus like she was a dog. "Here, Gus!" he called, then whistled the way I'd heard Finch call for his dogs in the past.

Maybe Gus was hiding inside. I stepped into the trailer, flipped on the light, and cursed.

The place had been trashed. Someone had emptied out every drawer and pulled all my possessions from closets, shelves, and storage spaces. Who did this? And why?

What were they looking for?

I picked up a drawer and slid it back into its spot. I gathered up eating and cooking utensils and dumped them in the sink to be washed later. I found a couple of julep cups on the floor and held them up to Luke. "They obviously weren't looking for valuables."

He scoffed. "Those would have been the *first* items I would have taken."

Despite the circumstances, I was thankful we could keep the banter light. It kept me from panicking.

I went to my bedroom. My clothes were all over the bed and on the floor. My sheets had been stripped away, and my mattress was sliced in several spots, as were the pillows, their insides pulled completely out.

"Whatever they were looking for… they thought I would put it in the pillows?"

"Faith, do you keep any of your crime scene photos here? It's conceivable someone might want those. I know you're not supposed to, but maybe you keep a backup?"

"I don't. I upload them to the server, and then delete my—" I stopped abruptly, then turned to my closet.

"What?" Luke said. "Do you know what they were searching for?"

"I'm afraid so."

I pulled out what few items that were left inside my closet, then popped open the secret compartment in the floor.

The box was still there. They hadn't found it.

But who would even have known it was here? Or what was in it?

And what, specifically, were they after? My copy of the crime scene photos didn't even include the photo of the leash. Would they be interested in the journals? They would include a description of the needlepoint gifts Leah had given us all for Christmas that year. I wasn't sure.

I removed the lid and verified that everything was still inside.

"You going to tell me what that is?" Luke asked.

Flashing police lights shone through the windows and tires crunched on gravel. And then I heard Gus's soft cry. The cat leapt up the steps and into the trailer.

"There you are!" I stepped around Luke and picked up Gus. "Don't you ever scare me like that again!" As I scratched the back of Gus's ears, she meowed and rubbed her face against mine. "Did you see who did this?" I asked her.

"I'm glad Gus is safe," Luke said in a low voice. "But do you want the police to see what's in that box?" He nodded toward the container, and his tone suggested that he knew it would be best that we kept its contents between us for now.

"Not yet," I said. "But if you'll help me make a quick report and give me a place to stay… I'll show you what I think someone was after."

"Deal. I might even let you bring your cat." Again he kept things light and comfortable between us, this time with a grin.

I returned the smile. "I saw your face when you realized she was missing. You like Gus."

"I like *you*," Luke said. "And I figure your cat is part of the package."

We went out to greet the police officer. It took twenty

minutes to give him our statements. I knew he wouldn't take fingerprints—it's usually not worth the trouble. In fact, police tend to get rather irritated when victims of break-ins insist on fingerprinting, then get upset when police leave behind a huge mess and find nothing usable.

And I certainly wasn't going to ask for prints. I didn't need them. I was fairly certain I already knew who had broken into my trailer.

THIRTY-ONE

Safely in Coop's warm barn apartment, Luke handed me a mismatched pair of bowls so that I could feed and water Gus.

"Thanks for letting us both crash here," I said.

"I'm just glad the two of you are okay. Now tell me what's in the box."

I straightened at his direct tone, then went over to the box I had set on the long farm table. I took out the old family photos and set them aside. "These are from my childhood," I said. "The few photos I could find in Aunt Leah's collection. Most of my childhood went up in flames with the fire."

His face softened with pity, a look I hated. I think he knew it, because he quickly got back to business. "What else? Surely someone didn't break into your home for baby photos."

"No, I don't believe they did." I tucked the journals into the bottom of the box, then pulled out the crime scene photos and set them on the table. "But they might have broken in for these." I pulled the photo from Ethan out of

225

my coat pocket and tossed it on top of the others. "Or more likely, this one."

He flipped through the stack. "These are from the night your mom died. Where did you get these? When we talked to the prosecutor, they couldn't produce them—system glitch or something."

"Ethan had a copy. It's part of the exculpatory evidence. He got it through... back channels." I was deliberately vague; there was no point telling him I had stolen most of these photos, and though I didn't like Tabitha Green, I wasn't about to rat her out specifically. She had helped uncover the truth, after all.

"And this one?" Luke asked, holding up the late addition. "You seem to think this one is significant?"

I looked down at the floor, then back up at Luke. He waited patiently for me to say something. Or maybe he was processing through his own thoughts and conclusions.

"Okay..." he said. "How about we start with a different question. Why did you call me tonight? Why not Finch? Or your uncle? Or even Chief Reid? He seems rather protective of you."

"I don't think protective is the right word," I said. I looked toward the windows. They were dark, and you couldn't see anything on the other side of them. I always hated the thought of someone being able to see inside windows that I couldn't see out of. Too many scary movies as a child, I supposed.

"Come on, Faith. Give me something." Luke lifted his hands then dropped them in frustration. "Surely by now you trust me."

I fidgeted with my hands. "That's why I called you," I said softly. "I do trust you."

"Then tell me what's special about this photo."

"I'm not really sure," I lied. It wasn't that I didn't trust him—at least, that's what I tried to convince myself—but I needed to first talk to Uncle Henry about the photo. If I was wrong about the conclusion I had drawn, I would ruin what was left of my family.

I approached Luke. I took the photo from his hands and set it on top of the others. I let my eyes drift slowly from his chest, up to his eyes, then to his lips. "This case isn't going anywhere tonight." I moved closer.

When I bent my knee, it knocked against his leg. I slid my hands to his waist and stared at his chest.

He took in a deep breath. "What are you doing?" He grabbed my shoulders firmly, holding me in place. "Don't play games with me, Faith." His gaze narrowed.

I decided to leak out a little bit of truth. "I have thoughts—assumptions, really, but I need to be careful. What Ethan told me tonight… it could ruin someone's life. *If* it's true."

"Do you believe Ethan?"

"I believe he deserved to be let out of prison. I believe he wants to find out who put him there and who's trying to harm me now. And I believe he wants to know who murdered his father."

Luke relaxed his hold, so I moved in close again, sliding my hands to his back.

He wrapped his arms around me. "I want to find out who's trying to hurt you, too. Did Ethan, or do you, have any ideas who that might be? Assuming for a second that it's not actually Ethan."

I lifted my hand and placed my fingers over his lips. "No more talk tonight."

I could see the torment in his eyes. I was starting to see that this man might actually care about me as much as he cared about finding a killer. He was trying to do the right thing—but what was that?

I let my hands roam up his back, to his shoulders, and down his arms. I let them linger along his hips, then moved them around to the front of his body. I knew the moment I had him, and there was no turning back.

His lips crushed against mine. He kissed me hard with intent and heat. His hands slipped under my shirt, touching my waist, my back, and continuing to roam.

I lifted his sweater over his head, and he returned the favor. We left a trail of clothing as we stumbled to the spiral staircase. He grabbed my hand and led me upstairs.

When we got to the top, he finished undressing me, and we fell into bed, leaving the details of a killer for another day.

It didn't take long for Luke to fall asleep after we'd made love. I got up, dressed, and using a dim lamp, I got to work on his evidence board. Gus sat on the table, cleaning herself.

I placed the photo of the dog leash next to the other evidence in my mother's murder. By itself it didn't prove anything, but it was enough for me to question everything I'd ever believed about my family—and it broke my heart in the process. It was a miracle I was holding my emotions together at all. My mind was working overtime to come up with reasons the leash didn't mean what I thought it meant.

I pushed those emotions aside, and studied the board.

Luke was a good investigator. He had boxes of files stacked against the wall, yet he had managed to transform the copious information into a concise timeline of twelve years of cases, making notes and drawing links. Some of the notes were clearly an attempt to find commonalities among the cases. He had drawn lines between a few of the cases, but had come up short with others.

I zeroed in on a case from two years ago, in a town just outside of Knoxville, in which the parents of a nine-year-old boy, Connor Bale, were murdered. Luke had written on a pink Post-It: *victim of molestation by Catholic priest.* According to a newspaper article pinned just above, the parents had known about the molestation for months. Even when the priest was arrested for child pornography, the parents didn't report the molestation of their son, because they feared what it would do to them socially and within their Catholic parish. It was ultimately the boy's pediatrician who reported the possible molestation to authorities—and then, under police interrogation, the mother broke down and admitted the truth.

That followed the pattern of some of the other cases. Parents who were aware of an inappropriate sexual relationship involving their child, but who remained silent about it.

Other cases had a slightly different pattern. News reports suggested sexual abuse of a minor, but there was no indication that the murder victims had known about that abuse. Yet I suspected they *did* know—in every case. Because that was the killer's motive. To punish those who knew. Those who knew and said nothing.

But that raised another question: if the sexual abuse didn't make the news until *after* the murders… how could the killer have known about the abuse? And how could the killer have known the victims were staying silent?

I followed one of Luke's strings from the newspaper article to a yellow Post-It note: *Pediatrician: Dr. Littleton, Lexington.* "Lexington" was circled.

Why had those parents driven their little boy all the way to Lexington to see a doctor?

I went carefully through the dates of all the cases, but this time, I did so with a fresh eye. I grabbed an aqua Post-It pad, since that color had not been used yet, made my own notes, and stuck them in the center of any case that I could add information to.

Then I stood back and looked at my handiwork.

As I examined the timeline—and at the horrible truth it revealed—I began to cry. Uncontrollable but silent tears streamed down my face.

I did one more thing. I pinned a piece of twine to the board.

It stretched from the picture of the dog leash... to the photograph of Finch.

THIRTY-TWO

I left before Luke woke. I left my journals on the table, key pages marked with Post-Its, and added a note: *Thanks for letting me borrow your car. I'll be back as soon as I can. Everything is explained on your timeline and in these journals.*

He'd be angry that I took his vehicle without waking him, but he'd forgive me when he saw my contribution to his evidence board.

However, I would never forgive myself for what I was about to do to my family. A family that had been through so much. A family that had worked so hard to put itself back together after the fire, the deaths, the trial.

I thought back to the early days after Finch and I finished up our schooling—vet school for him, undergraduate for me—and came back to town. Finch set up his practice in Paynes Creek to be near me. Aubrey, who was estranged from her parents, supported him emotionally and financially while he got his practice up and running. It didn't take long; his natural charm and easygoing demeanor led to near-instant success. Within a year his fledgling practice was well in the black, and Aubrey was continuing her work at the behavioral health center in Lexington. She'd started there as an intern, and then became a full-time therapist.

And they both assumed I'd move in with them. But I didn't want to cramp the newlywed couple just getting their adult lives in order. I purchased the Airstream, remodeled it, and moved back onto the farm I grew up on. Most people thought I was crazy—and maybe I was. But I had more good memories than bad ones on that farm.

And I remembered everything. I had vivid memories of every single thing I had done. Everything anyone had done to me.

Everything they had ever said to me.

And right now, I wished I didn't.

By the time I pulled into Uncle Henry's and Aunt Leah's driveway, my hands were shaking, my breathing was shallow, and a cold sweat had broken out over my entire body. I walked carefully up the sidewalk to my aunt and uncle's modest white clapboard house. Aunt Leah's bright yellow mums, scarred by the snow and ice, were starting to turn brown and die.

I didn't bother to knock. I pushed through the front door and stood inside the foyer, my feet suddenly heavy with dread.

Aunt Leah walked out from the kitchen, wiping her hands on a dish towel. "Hi, Faith, honey. You want some breakfast?" She paused mid-wipe and studied me. "You okay?"

I didn't answer—I couldn't. I only stared at her.

She called out to Uncle Henry. "Henry? Come quick."

I heard Uncle Henry's heavy footsteps coming down

the stairs. "What is it?" he asked in a pleasant voice. But when he saw me, his cheeks drooped. "What's wrong?"

"I've seen the evidence," I said in a low voice. My eyes bored into Uncle Henry's.

He remained silent.

I said it louder. "I've seen the evidence that freed Ethan from prison and convinced the commonwealth's attorney to not even bother with a retrial."

He took a couple of steps toward me, and I instinctively backed away. This wouldn't go away with a hug or a kind touch to my arm.

I looked down at my fidgety hands, then up at Uncle Henry. Moisture filled my eyes. "He didn't do it." I paused, gauging his reaction. He remained stoic. "But you've always known that."

"What's she talking about?" Aunt Leah asked.

Something akin to agony flitted over Uncle Henry's face. "Let's go sit down."

"I don't want to sit down!" I shouted. "I want you to tell me the *truth*! Right here. Right now!"

"Faith, honey. I will tell you the truth. But I need to sit down to do it."

Aunt Leah, visibly shaken, said nothing as she followed Uncle Henry toward the kitchen. I walked behind them. I stretched my fingers wide, then curled them into fists. My heart was racing with anxiety like a jackrabbit fleeing a fox.

We'd had very few serious conversations over the years, but they almost always occurred at Aunt Leah's kitchen table.

Apparently Aunt Leah had been making a country breakfast. She walked to the stove and began flipping the bacon and eggs.

"Turn the stove off and sit down, Leah," Uncle Henry ordered.

"Let me finish this," she said, clearly trying to mask her fear by staying busy. "If we're going to have a serious talk, we should at least eat."

Uncle Henry approached his wife, took the spatula, and set it aside. He turned off the gas burners, pushed the pans aside, and placed his hands on her shoulders. "I need you to sit down." He leaned in and kissed her forehead.

He then walked over and pulled out a chair for her. When she was seated, he sat in the neighboring seat and nodded toward another chair.

I shook my head. "I don't want to sit."

Aunt Leah stayed quiet. I wondered if she already suspected part of the truth. Perhaps she even knew it, all of it, and had been expecting this day would come.

I removed my phone from my coat pocket and pulled up a photograph I'd taken of Luke's evidence board. I zoomed in on the photo I'd tacked onto the board and slid the phone in front of Uncle Henry. "That photo is from the crime scene." I stuffed my hands back in my pockets. "Ethan thinks that's your leash—the one you used for Scout. But it isn't, is it? That's Finch's leash for Sally Brown, his new puppy at the time. He was at the house that night, wasn't he?"

Uncle Henry closed his eyes. His head fell forward. "Where did you find this?"

"Does it matter? Had Ethan's attorney received this photo—as required by law—it might not have changed the verdict. But it would at least have convinced detectives to explore the idea that someone else killed Mom and Eli." I leaned into the table. "But you know what *would* have changed the verdict? The witness statement and the time-stamped video that proved he couldn't be guilty. Had that evidence not been buried, or had evidence not been planted in his car, he would never have been arrested, let alone convicted."

I looked Uncle Henry right in the eye. "Tell me this: after Finch killed Mom, whose idea was it to burn the evidence? Yours or Finch's?"

"What is she talking about?" Aunt Leah asked. Her voice was elevated a full octave, bordering on hysteria. She had remained quiet while she listened to me rant, occasionally looking at her husband's face.

But he didn't dare look away from me, even as he placed a hand over his wife's. "Why don't you let me talk to Faith alone. And then we'll——"

"Henry Ballard Nash! You will not manhandle me in my own kitchen. You will tell me the truth. And if that means I need to sit here and listen quietly, then I will."

Uncle Henry nodded, defeat etched in every line in his face. "You have to understand, Faith. It was an accident. Your brother only meant to protect you."

My hand went instinctively to my mouth as I smothered a sob. That was when I finally pulled out a chair and sat, if only to avoid fainting. My own brother had murdered our mother.

Aunt Leah grabbed Uncle Henry's arm and stared at him in disbelief for a brief eternity. "What in God's name are you saying?"

He turned to her. "I'm so sorry. I've only kept one secret from you over the years. And I only did it to protect our family. Our Finch only wanted to protect his sister. It was a terrible accident, but he killed his own mother. And Eli. And Lord help me, I helped him destroy the evidence."

Aunt Leah stared at her husband. And as the devastating truth set in, she began to weep.

THIRTY-THREE

Uncle Henry helped Aunt Leah upstairs and gave her some anti-anxiety medicine to calm her down. When he returned, he took a seat beside me.

I fisted my hands on the table, fighting back tears. My brother had killed my mother, and then he'd allowed our stepbrother to take the fall. The grief and anger coursing through me was overwhelming.

But I needed to be brave. Not only for myself, but for my brother, who had barely been an adult himself when he did what he did. It was now time to learn why.

I faced my uncle. Instead of looking like the weight of his guilt was piled on his shoulders, he actually looked relieved.

"I've been carrying this burden for twelve years," he said. He hung his head. "I'm tired. And I'm old."

"Do you regret your part in it?" It was a simple question, but it was also a way of stalling, before we got to the question I really wanted to ask. *Why did my brother kill our mom?*

Uncle Henry angled his head and studied me for a

second. "Not for one second." His voice was certain. "Your stepbrother was obsessed with you."

"Obsessed with me?" I said. "What are you talking about?"

"That boy watched your every move. He made sure no other boy ever looked at you, let alone asked you out. The two of you were inseparable, and I watched how uncomfortable you became your junior year."

"You saw that?"

"Everyone saw it," Uncle Henry said. "And one night, Eli was out at some town event and he mentioned how convenient it would be if you and Ethan got married someday. He might have been joking, I don't know, but when Finch's friends told him about it, he became irate. He talked it over with Aubrey, since she was on her way to becoming a psychologist. And she encouraged him to talk to you about your relationship with Ethan. Which he did, right?"

"I told him Ethan was my best friend."

"That's not all you told him."

"No," I said, shaking my head. "It wasn't. I told him that Ethan thought he was in love with me and that I wasn't sure how to handle it without hurting the rest of the family."

"Finch asked some of his friends to keep an eye on you —friends who were still in Paynes Creek. One of them reported back that Ethan had come on to you at a party after drinking too much, and that you had to shove him away. People were talking about the two of you."

"They were," I recalled. "I hated it. But I knew we'd go to different colleges eventually, and he'd lose interest in me. And the gossip would die."

"Not according to Finch," Uncle Henry said. "He and Aubrey agreed that your relationship with Ethan was highly inappropriate, and that Finch needed to step in, since your mother and stepfather clearly weren't."

"Step in? But he didn't just step in, he——" My words caught in my throat, and I struggled to breathe. None of this was a reason for Finch to kill my mother.

I barely whispered my next words. "What did he do, Uncle Henry?" But what I wanted to ask was: *What did he become?*

"Finch came home that night. He wanted to confront Ethan. And he wanted to tell your mother and Eli that they were making a big mistake by not putting a stop to Ethan's behavior. And that joking about a relationship that you didn't want, and that many thought was immoral, was wrong. He wanted for all of you to have a conversation, and to get Ethan the help he needed."

Uncle Henry took a deep breath. "But no one was there when he got home. So he went through Ethan's things. He found a box of photos... of you."

"What kind of photos?"

"Photos from prom... with your dates cut out. Photos he took of you while you were sleeping. Photos clearly taken from a distance. It was obvious he was stalking you."

"Did you see these pictures?" I asked.

Uncle Henry shook his head. "Finch only told me about them."

"When? After you burned down my home, or before?" I stood and leaned over him. "When did you decide to burn my house, the evidence, *and* my mother's body?"

"Faith..."

"Finish the story. What did Finch do after he found the photos?"

Uncle Henry's face fell again. His cheeks were flushed, and he appeared to be overheating. "Aw, honey. You don't need to hear the rest."

"I have to hear the whole story."

He took in another deep breath and let it out. "Eli and your mom returned home. They'd been out to dinner. Finch confronted them. And when he told them that he suspected Ethan was sexually assaulting you, Eli laughed."

I took in a sharp breath. "He laughed?"

"He laughed and told Finch that you and Ethan weren't doing anything that two teenagers hadn't been doing for thousands of years."

I narrowed my gaze. "What about Mom? Was she okay with what Ethan was doing?"

"Your mom tried to pass it off as if nothing inappropriate had happened. She told Finch she was confident you hadn't taken the relationship too far. But then... but then Eli told Finch that he thought it would be great if you had."

I gasped. "*What?*"

"He claimed that his son would be the best thing that could ever happen to you. That Ethan would be the only man who could ever accept you for the way your mind and memories worked. So Finch punched him."

"He was defending me," I said.

"He was," Uncle Henry agreed. "But Eli fought back. He said some things to make Finch even angrier. And Finch lost control. He spun Eli around and put him in a chokehold until he could no longer breathe. Your mom tried to stop him. She pulled at Finch's arm, but Finch, purely out of reflex, shoved her away. Your mom fell backwards and hit her head on the edge of the countertop. Her death was a terrible accident."

"Accident?" I said.

"Finch lost control."

"He was angry. Because the people who were supposed

to protect me… didn't." I was talking to myself more than to Uncle Henry, but he heard and understood.

"I know what you're thinking, but you're wrong. Finch is no serial killer. He's not even an arsonist. I committed the arson that night. To protect *him*."

"No." Tears were now streaming down my face, but I was too angry to succumb to the grief I was feeling. "You did more than that. You didn't just protect Finch—you framed Ethan. You made sure that he would be charged and convicted. You sent an innocent man to prison!"

"Innocent?" Uncle Henry said. "You're calling a boy who raped my seventeen-year-old niece *innocent*? He deserved to go to prison."

His words knocked the breath out of me like a punch to the gut. I stumbled backwards. Uncle Henry started to stand, but I lifted a hand. "Don't." My eyes met his. "How did you know?"

"In the hospital, your Aunt Leah overheard you talking to Ethan from your hospital bed. You said you'd never forgive him for what he did to you that night and that he would never lay another hand on you. She could hear the sheer terror in your voice, and she knew. She knew that he had raped you."

The room began to spin. I grabbed the back of a chair. My darkest secret—one I thought would stay secret forever —was already known by the people closest to me. And they had said nothing.

"But you had *already* decided to pin the fire on Ethan. You planted evidence to make sure he looked guilty."

Uncle Henry shook his head. "No. I didn't plant the gas cans until after that. When Finch called me that night —right after he found the photos—he was so angry. I went over there immediately, but by the time I got there, it was too late. Eli and your mother were already dead. Your brother was beside himself. Inconsolable. So I found the gas cans in the barn, and I burned the evidence by burning the house. And that was all.

"But then your Aunt Leah discovered what Ethan had done. And then… yes, I planted the gas cans in Ethan's car. And since I was in charge of the arson investigation, it was easy to make sure Detective Reid saw what I needed him to see. I made sure that boy got what he deserved."

"Did Chief know Ethan was innocent?"

"He didn't care once I told him Ethan had raped you."

"And then the two of you buried the evidence that would've proven his innocence."

Why had I never allowed Ethan to tell me his side of things? If he had, I would have tried to help him— wouldn't I? Or was it unfair to ask that question of the twenty-nine-year-old version of me? It was the seventeen-year-old Faith Day that had just been raped.

"How did you figure it out?" Uncle Henry asked in a quiet voice.

I swiped at the moisture on my face. "The photo. One of Aunt Leah's leashes *is* hanging there. Ethan thought it was your leash for Scout. But I recognized it as Finch's leash for Sally Brown." Aunt Leah had used the Auburn University colors of blue and orange, because Finch had just been accepted to the vet school there. "Then I just started thinking about the timing of everything, and why Finch didn't come home immediately. And I realized, he had come home. He just didn't come see me in the hospital right away."

With my hands on the back of a chair, I bent over at my waist and stared down at the floor. The chain reaction that had begun the moment I realized that Finch's leash was left on the hook of our childhood home had been overwhelming.

"Who have you told?" he asked.

Technically, I'd told no one. But Ethan was close to the truth, and I'd left Luke enough details to put it all together. To not just connect Finch to this crime, but to the others. I had used Post-Its to mark down where Finch was during each of the crimes on Luke's wall—and he had been out of town for every crime that had occurred after we both moved back to Paynes Creek, except of course for the ones that had occurred right here in town. I wasn't able to pin down Finch's whereabouts in the earlier crimes, because we were both still in school, but it was enough.

It would take time for Luke to accumulate hard evidence that proved Finch had become a monster leading a double life—devoted husband and animal-lover most days, but cold-blooded killer and vigilante when the mood struck. But Luke would do it.

"Why do you want to know?" I asked.

"I want to know how long I have to get my affairs in order," Uncle Henry said. "I'm assuming you've told the FBI agent. Can I call Finch and Aubrey and warn them?"

"Warn *them*?" I asked. "Aubrey knows what he did?" I couldn't believe what I was hearing. "How can she live with that?" I waved the question off. "It doesn't matter. I hate you and Finch for doing what you did, and if Aubrey knew and said nothing, I hate her too. Your idea of protecting me sent a kid to prison for life. Yes, you should prepare yourself. And God help Aunt Leah."

THIRTY-FOUR

I slipped behind the wheel of Luke's SUV and knew that my life was about to change again. But worse than that, I was about to lose my brother—the brother I thought I knew so well. Turns out I didn't know him at all.

And then there was Aubrey. How could she act like my friend—my sister—all these years, knowing all the while that my own brother had killed our mother?

All this time, my entire family, except for Aunt Leah, had clung to the lie that Ethan was guilty. When he was released from prison, they claimed it was a mistake. And they *knew* that I had been raped, yet all along, through all those years I spent in therapy, not once did my family let me know that I didn't have to suffer alone. That I could talk to *them*.

Except, in a way, Aubrey. She had set me up with a really good psychologist. Perhaps that was her way of reaching out. I couldn't talk to her, but she made sure I could talk to *someone*. I wish she had just told me the truth—but she had done the next best thing. She had tried.

And now it was time for me to return that favor. I was

about to send my brother to prison, and destroy Aubrey's life. And she had a baby on the way. I at least owed it to her to go warn her. To tell her about the storm that was coming.

I was driving down Main Street when an orchestra of police sirens erupted behind me. As I pulled over to let them pass, I saw it wasn't local squad cars, but a caravan of black SUVs with police lights in their front windows. That could only mean Luke had seen my notes. They were on their way to Finch's veterinary office. To arrest my brother.

As I watched each car speed by, I flipped through memories of my childhood. We'd started out as a happy family—Mom, Dad, Finch and me. Until Dad died, changing us all, it was a pretty good life. A great life.

And now my brother was about to make headlines—in the worst way.

My phone buzzed in the passenger seat. I looked over and saw Luke's name on the screen. I answered. "Hi," I said softly.

"I don't know what to say."

"You don't have to say anything."

"Are you okay?"

"No," I said honestly. "But I'll find my way again." I watched the taillights of the feds fade in the distance. "Sorry about taking your car. I'll leave it at Coop's. I'd like to pick up Gus."

"I wish I could meet you there."

"It's okay. I need to be alone. Besides, you have a job to do, Special Agent Justice." I paused. He would have to interrogate my brother, hoping to get him to confess to a string of murders. "Finch didn't mean to kill Eli and Mom," I added weakly. "Uncle Henry said that Finch lost control and killed Eli in a rage. And Mom's death was an accident. She fell." I stared out the window at icicles dripping from a couple of the storefronts. "I guess it's cliché to say, 'He led such a quiet, simple life. He was a family man. Went to church on Sundays.'"

"Are all those things true?" Luke asked.

"Yeah." I laughed under my breath. "I saw your agents driving past. Picking up my brother, I assume."

He hesitated. "I'm watching video of them arriving at the vet clinic now—live feed from one of the officers' body cams."

"And Uncle Henry?"

"He called the police station. He's turning himself in. We've also temporarily relieved Chief Reid of his duties while we question his involvement."

I sniffed loudly. "What about Aubrey? I assume you'll be detaining her for interviews?"

"A couple of uniforms should be on their way to her soon. And an evidence response team is on their way from the FBI office in Louisville. "

"One thing still doesn't make sense," I said. "I don't think Finch is the person who's been harassing me."

"Why do you say that?"

"For one, whoever it was snuck into my trailer while I was sleeping, and with Gus there. But Gus always screams and hisses when Finch comes in. To Gus, Finch is the evil man that spayed her and gives her shots. For another, Finch could easily carry me. He wouldn't have needed to drag me through the snow to the fire that night. And finally... why? Why would he do any of this?"

"Good points." Luke seemed to be thinking. "I'm going to keep someone stationed at your home."

"Thank you."

"And we'll need you to come in later today or tomorrow. You've given me enough information to begin the initial interrogations and interviews, but I would like to talk some things over with you."

"It doesn't seem real," I said.

"Faith, I'm really sorry."

"Me too."

***

Finch's and Aubrey's house was dark when I arrived. I wondered where Aubrey was—she was supposed to be staying in bed. I hoped she wasn't out shopping for baby accessories again. I would hate for her to hear this devastating news while out and about.

I knew an evidence team was on its way, and I wondered if I would be breaking any sort of laws if I went in. But I did have a key. It wasn't breaking and entering.

My curiosity got the best of me. I grabbed my camera and let myself in.

I stepped lightly down the hallway to their bedroom, just in case Aubrey was there and asleep. But the bed was made, and the room looked like it had just been freshly cleaned. I walked over to their dresser and looked at a framed photo from their wedding. Finch was smiling into the camera, and Aubrey's head was thrown back, her face full of laughter. They got married at their church and had a reception in the gardens of a local historic home. It had been a beautiful sunny day. Now it only brought me sadness.

I left the bedroom and went to Finch's home office. He often brought his paperwork home so that he could be with Aubrey while she cooked dinner. The office was not tidy at all; paper was strewn about the desk. I recognized some of the reports. It appeared Finch had been working on his clinic's accounting. Beneath the reports was a folder, with the edges of newspaper peeking out from inside.

I didn't know what I was looking for, but I felt like I was examining a crime scene. And I wanted to preserve things for the evidence team. I pulled out my camera and snapped a couple of photos, then pulled on a pair of latex gloves, which I always kept in my camera bag. Very carefully, I moved Finch's accounting reports to the side and opened the manila folder.

Inside was a stack of articles. Some were cut out from an actual newspaper, others were printed from the internet. The top article was about the two recent fires—the Reynolds fire and the Porter fire. The one beneath that was an online article about the Midland fire, the one involving the Siegelmans. That was the one where I'd spotted the dog tags that matched the tags from Finch's practice.

I let my eyes close for a moment. When I first noticed the dog tag, it was such a tiny detail. Now it loomed large.

I flipped to the bottom of the stack. This article was also about a fire, but not one that was on Luke's evidence board. It was an old one—it had occurred later in the same year that Eli and my mom were killed.

The article was dated Monday, November twenty-fourth. Three days before Thanksgiving. The headline read: *UK Calls Off Classes to Mourn Loss of 10 Students in Fraternity House Fire*.

I remembered that fire. Investigators immediately suspected arson. Gasoline had been poured on the stairs leading to the second floor, and the boys in the house were forced to jump out of second-story windows. Other boys were trapped when the fire spread.

Had Finch started this fire too?

I thought back to November twenty-fourth. Ethan's trial was in full swing. I went every day to watch the testimony. Finch was on break, and joined me in court that day.

The fire had occurred early Sunday morning the day before. Finch had come home for break on Saturday night. We had a family dinner, and he stayed over with us at Uncle Henry's and Aunt Leah's.

Which meant...

He couldn't have started this fire.

Thoughts and memories were coming at me fast. I knew the evidence response team would be here soon, and I suddenly felt an impossible need to prove that my brother *wasn't* a serial killer.

I took photographs of the articles, then I scanned the rest of the room. Finch kept his veterinary records at the clinic, but he and Aubrey had a wide two-drawer filing cabinet that served as a credenza.

I opened the top drawer and flipped through it. It was filled with personal financial files—brokerage statements, bank statements, tax returns, medical files. I closed it and opened the lower drawer. This one was filled with manila folders. And on each tab was a file label with a name in bold letters.

Most of them meant nothing to me. But I recognized some of the names.

Porter.

Reynolds.

Siegelman.

Sims.

These were patient files. Aubrey had been counseling these young girls.

Then I spotted another file label. Bale. The victim of the Catholic priest from Knoxville. Luke had noted that Connor's parents brought Connor to a Lexington pediatrician. That was a long way to go for a doctor... unless they were trying to keep Connor's troubles a secret.

Aubrey specialized in counseling victims of sexual assault.

All of these victims were her clients.

The room began to spin.

I quickly pulled my phone from my pocket and called Luke. My call went to voicemail.

"Luke, call me. I need to know: How many of the victims of sexual assault or sexual harassment were in counseling? And where did they get the counseling? Call me." I hung up and placed my phone in my back pocket.

"Hi, Faith."

I spun around at the sound of Aubrey's voice. But something hit me over the head as I did, and everything went dark.

THIRTY-FIVE

I woke to the smell of gasoline. My head ached when I tried to lift it. My hands were tied behind my back. I was on the floor in Finch's office.

I tried to look around the room for something to help me cut through what felt like thick twine around my wrists. When I moved, I felt something hard in my back pocket.

My phone.

Fumbling, I pulled it from my pocket. I pushed myself up, felt for the side button on the phone, then twisted my head to see the time. I hadn't been unconscious long, and Luke's evidence response team still hadn't arrived, nor had any officers come to talk to Aubrey.

Where the hell were they?

I placed my finger on the phone's home button to wake it. A list of numbers popped up on the screen—the last numbers I had dialed. I pressed Luke's name.

I could hear his voice, but I didn't want Aubrey to hear me, so I put the phone on the floor, then lay down with my head next to it, so I could whisper into it. When I got close enough, I could tell it was his voicemail again.

"Luke, Aubrey is the serial killer," I whispered, praying he could hear me. "Aubrey has me tied up at her house. I can smell gasoline."

I heard footsteps approaching, and I used my head to push the phone under the desk.

Aubrey appeared in the doorway. She was wearing one of Finch's winter coats, and her hair was tucked up under a baseball cap.

"At my fire pit," I said. "When I spotted you. I thought it was an overweight man, but it was you."

She cocked her head like she wasn't sure what I was talking about. "Well, that's not very nice. Are you saying this baby is making me look fat?"

I struggled to sit up, and leaned against the desk. "All those years ago when I accused you of looking into my therapist's file... You denied it, but I was right. That's how you knew about the daisies that you left inside my trailer."

"I was only trying to help you, Faith. After what Ethan had done to you, I wanted to be there for you." She sounded so sincere, yet she still hadn't quite admitted to any wrongdoing.

I was seeing a side to Aubrey I'd never seen before.

"I don't understand why you've got me tied up," I said. "Uncle Henry already admitted that Finch killed Eli and accidentally caused Mom's death."

"Oh he did. And the guilt of that nearly killed *him*." She lifted a hand and examined her manicure like she didn't have a care in the world. "But I helped him through it. I made him understand that it was all truly an accident, and that he did you a favor by letting that rapist take the fall for the crime. Rapists deserve to be punished. But do you know the type of person I truly despise?"

"Who's that?" I wriggled my hands, trying to break the twine or slip a hand free, but failed.

"The enablers. Men and women who protect the guilty. I mean, rapists, sexual harassers, abusers of little girls and boys? They deserve to be punished for their crimes. But those who stand by and *let* those innocent victims be abused? As far as I'm concerned, they're every bit as guilty."

I remembered the article about the fraternity house fire. "What happened to you, Aubrey?"

"Your brother is amazing, you know." Tears filled her eyes. "He was there for me when no one else was. My parents sure as hell weren't. 'You shouldn't have dressed like that, Aubrey. How much did *you* have to drink, Aubrey?' They might as well have told me I deserved it. That I had asked for it." Her voice grew louder. "Those boys raped me!"

I closed my eyes. "I'm so sorry," I said, and I meant it.

"So I burned their house down," she nearly sang.

She wore a smug grin. I didn't need to know anything more. I realized the mistake I had made when I stared at Luke's evidence board. I had been so focused on Finch's travel schedule, I had failed to note that when Finch went out of town, Aubrey usually went out of town, too—on girls' trips with her Pistol Packin' Mamas group. And she was the one who scheduled those trips; I'd been over here one night when she was planning one.

"Why did you break into my trailer?"

Ignoring my question, she rubbed her belly. "He's moving around. Want to feel?"

With every minute that passed without the FBI knocking on the door, the smell of gasoline worsened, and my worry rose.

"Yes," I answered.

She took a step toward me, then stopped. "Oh, I guess you can't," she said.

"You can untie me, Aubrey. You think I would hurt your baby? That's my niece or nephew growing inside of you. I love that baby already."

"That's why I needed your journal."

So she *had* broken into my trailer. And the rest of it? Had she started the fires in my fire pit? Hit me over the head and dragged me through the snow? She hadn't admitted to any of that.

"Because you wanted to see if I'd written about your unborn child?" I asked. "Because I didn't. I haven't written in my journals in years."

"I needed to know if you would be a good aunt to my child. I wanted to know the truth about you."

"What truth is that?"

"I wanted to know what happened between you and Ethan all those years ago. I know he raped you, and he shouldn't have done that, but I wanted to know if you encouraged him. If you were to blame for his obsession with you. My parents always said I was to blame, and part of me wonders if that was true. But I also wanted to know if you were a little tease to Ethan."

Her suggestion was like a knife in my heart. It didn't matter what else I might have done, I had expressly told Ethan "no" that night.

"You and I didn't deserve what happened to us," I said. "I don't care what your parents said, you didn't deserve to be raped. No one deserves that. Let me help you now. We can help each other. Finch didn't mean to kill Mom and Eli. The judge will understand that." I didn't think for one second Aubrey would fall for that garbage, but I was desperately stalling, praying the cops would show up.

My phone buzzed under the desk. I closed my eyes, knowing Aubrey could hear it, too. It was the sound of texts coming through. At least three, one after the other.

"Where's that coming from?" She bent down and spotted my phone. Then she knelt on all fours and grabbed it from under the desk. By the time she struggled to stand up, she was breathing hard. The baby had to be pressing on her diaphragm.

"It's Agent Justice," she said. "He's sending a uniform to pick you up at your trailer. And the ERT unit is in town and is following a squad car to our house."

Luke obviously hadn't listened to my message yet.

Aubrey looked up. "Looks like our time is up, Faith. I'm sorry that it has to come to this. But if it hadn't been for you, no one would have figured out that Finch was the one who killed your mom. And now you have to pay for taking my child's father from him."

"It's a boy?" I said, trying to keep her talking. "You said 'him.'"

"That's right." She smiled as she rubbed her stomach. "And I need strong, righteous people to teach him how to be a man with a solid moral compass who respects women. You just aren't one of those people, I'm afraid."

"What makes you say that?"

"People talk, Faith. And they like talking about you and Ethan. A reporter grabbed me coming out of the vet clinic the other day. Marla, I think? She had a lot of interesting things to say about you and Ethan. I think she's working on one of those prime-time real crime shows." She waved a hand. "It doesn't matter. You and I are out of time." She pulled a matchbook from her pocket—a matchbook from the Spotted Cat.

She backed slowly toward the doorway, then stopped. "Finch and I truly loved you, Faith. May you rest in peace."

She struck the match and dropped it on the floor.

The entire doorway burst into flames.

THIRTY-SIX

The flames spread quickly to the ceiling, extinguishing any hope I had of scooting or hopping my way out of the room. I rolled toward the windows, which looked out onto the back yard. I sat up, then used the wall to push myself to my feet. Wood blinds covered the windows. I shoved them to the side with my body.

The windows were locked, and I couldn't lift my hands high enough to unlock them.

I hopped over to a ladder-back chair, grabbed it with my bound hands, and hopped back over to the window, dragging the chair behind me.

Smoke had filled the room, and I couldn't even shield my face. Coughing, I climbed onto the chair and, with my back to the window, tried to unlock the window.

The flames were growing closer and the smoke was getting worse.

The lock was tight. I leaned forward to give my hands better access, and was able to twist the lock. But the motion threw me off balance, and I tipped the chair and fell hard on my right shoulder.

I took in a deep breath—the air was clear of smoke down here—then held it as I rose again. With one last, adrenaline-laced scream, I pushed open the window just enough for my body to fit through.

I rammed my head through first, pushing right through the screen, and fell onto the ground outside. I landed flat on my back with a grunt.

I could now hear distant sirens, and people yelling. I had nothing else left in me to scream, so I just rolled away from the house as far as I could. Behind me, flames now shot from the very window through which I had escaped. I clung to consciousness by a thread. The emotional and physical poundings of this past week were finally getting the best of me.

A man's voice. "Back here! Send the paramedics!"

Luke.

And then he was at my side. "Faith, can you hear me?"

I was lying on my stomach in the grass. My hands were still tied behind me.

I twisted my head just slightly. "What took you so long?"

He smiled down at me and flashed that look of pity I used to hate about him. He reached down to an ankle holster and pulled out a knife. When he held it up, he almost looked victorious. "Good thing I believe in carrying extra weapons."

"Good thing," I said.

The paramedics arrived seconds later. In short order, they had me on a gurney with an IV of fluids and an oxygen mask.

"Sir, we'll take her to Paynes Creek Memorial to get her checked out. You can meet her there."

Luke nodded, then touched my arm in that reassuring

way he always seemed to do. I had thought it was annoying at first, but now it was kind of growing on me.

I pulled the mask away. "Did you get her?" Just saying those words made tears spring to my eyes. I would be mourning the loss of my sister-in-law for the rest of my life.

"We got her."

THIRTY-SEVEN

I spent three days cleaning up my Airstream, securing all of my belongings in cabinets and drawers, and preparing the trailer and Gus for life on the road.

I said my goodbyes to Penelope. She was busy trying to hold the station together as an interim chief took over. It had been confirmed that when Chief Reid was the lead detective on my mother's case, he gave the assistant commonwealth's attorney the gas station video and agreed to "forget it existed" at trial.

Aunt Leah was taking everything hard, but she understood my need to get away. I promised to come back when the trials for my uncle, my brother, and his wife began. And she and I would do everything we could to see to it that Aubrey's and Finch's son was taken care of.

I was securing the trailer to the hitch on my SUV when I heard a vehicle come down the drive.

Gus slinked over and sat at my feet as I turned.

Luke climbed out of his vehicle and sauntered toward me. "Looks like I came just in time." He stuffed his hands in his pants pockets, leaving his thumbs hooked on the outside. "Which direction are you headed?"

"South," I said. "Thinking about making my way to the Florida Keys." Gus stood and circled between and around Luke's legs. "Looks like someone is going to miss you."

"Is she the only one?"

I tilted my head side to side, then smiled without answering.

"I'm meeting with prosecutors in three states the rest of the week," he said. "But then I have a few vacation days coming my way."

"You have my number, Special Agent."

He moved closer and placed his hands on my hips. Pulling me against his body, he leaned in and gave me a single soft kiss.

I snaked a hand behind his neck and into his hair. I pressed my lips against his, deeper this time—a kiss he wouldn't forget. When I pulled back just a little, our breaths marrying between us, I said, "Something to remember me by."

THIRTY-EIGHT

Three weeks passed. Luke had visited for one long weekend and promised to catch up with me again in the future.

I relived the horrible memories of the past month each and every day. But I also found joy in snorkeling, collecting bits of nature on long walks along the coast, and getting into a more artistic side of photography.

And hearing from Luke from time to time was nice.

Gus and I made friends in a few of the places where we hooked up the Airstream. We finally settled in a park in Long Key near Islamorada.

And tonight, I spent an evening with new friends. We grilled freshly caught fish over charcoal and consumed brightly colored rum drinks with umbrellas. When in Rome and all… And we laughed until well past midnight.

I drifted off to sleep with Gus curled up at my feet.

Later that night, I awoke to a strange noise. At first I thought it was my neighbors still enjoying their small campfire. But then I heard someone yell, "Fire!"

I sat up in bed and nearly lost my breath at the sight of candles lit on the shelf around my bed. One word escaped my lips.

"Ethan."

ABOUT THE AUTHOR

Heather Sunseri is a recovering CPA who began writing novels in order to escape the mundane life as a muggle. After twenty years in the corporate world, Heather decided to use her business savvy and curious mind to start a publishing business anchored by fictional stories. She is proof that one can be a numbers person and a creative... And that it's never too late (or too early) to get a do over.

Want to receive exclusive offers and stay on top of all the news in Heather Sunseri's fictional world? Sign up for Heather's VIP reader newsletter at heathersunseri.com. You can also connect with her in the following ways:

Heather Sunseri
P.O. Box 1264
Versailles, KY 40383
Website: https://heathersunseri.com
Email: heather@heathersunseri.com

Photo by Candace Sword

Made in the USA
Coppell, TX
19 January 2021

48453233R00156